CASEY'S SECRETS

A REBEL LUST TABOO NOVELLA

OPHELIA BELL

ANIMUS PRESS

Casey's Secrets

Published by Ophelia Bell
UNITED STATES

❀ Created with Vellum

PART I
SECRETS

"*I*s that clock right?" I asked my friend Sarah, pointing at the dashboard clock in her car. We'd been parked outside my house, deep in conversation for who knew how long already. I'd made such a point of making it home by curfew, I'd totally spaced that I needed to actually go inside before midnight for it to count. Now, the clock read "12:05" in accusatory bright orange.

"Yeah, it's right … What's the matter, Case?"

"Fuck! Fuck, fuck, fuck. I've gotta go. Max likes to wait up just to catch me breaking the rules. He's been a total jerk about it all year."

"Your stepdad's a super hot jerk, at least."

"You're not helping. I'll call you tomorrow, 'kay?"

I hustled out of her car and waved a quick farewell before jogging up the walkway. I took the steps two at a time onto the front porch. The living room lights were on, which didn't bode well. I didn't care how hot Sarah thought my stepdad was—ever since I'd turned eighteen he'd suddenly turned into an overbearing asshole about the "rules of the house." I could hear him now: "You may be an adult now, Casey, but as long as you continue living under my roof, you'll continue following my rules."

He was even worse whenever Mom was out of town on business, which was about a week out of every month, including this week. I'm not sure what had gotten into him. I missed the sweet guy who had taught me to ride a bike, who had built me a dollhouse before I got too old to play with dolls.

Now I dreaded even opening the door and having to deal with his critical scrutiny. The fact that he was probably the best looking man I'd ever known simply made things worse. The older I got, the more I recognized his purely sexual appeal. Why Mom had probably married him. And I hated understanding what it meant. I hated worse that he didn't seem to see me any differently, even though I'd grown up. I was still a little girl breaking the rules to him. But to me, he'd always been the man I wanted most, even if it meant loving him in secret.

I loved the guy even more in spite of his shift in behavior, and I hated disappointing him. Of course, the things he didn't know about me would probably make his head explode, like the tattoos and the piercings that I kept cleverly hidden.

My key slipped into the lock and I opened the door slowly, my pulse racing. I breathed a shaky sigh when I walked through the foyer and saw the living room empty. Only the vintage Tiffany lamp my mom loved was lit on one side table. The huge grandfather clock ticked away against the wall beneath the staircase.

Maybe I could get to my room before Dad realized I was ten minutes late. I could throw on my PJs and pretend I'd been there for a while and he wouldn't be any wiser.

The master bedroom door was closed at the end of the hall, no light shining beneath. That was a good sign. He'd probably gone to sleep. Maybe he'd relaxed a bit finally and decided to cut me some slack.

It didn't register that my own bedroom light was on until I rounded the doorframe and saw my dad sitting at the foot of my bed.

I stopped cold.

"You're late, Casey." His deep baritone accusation sent my heart back into arrhythmia territory.

"Just a few minutes," I said. "Seriously, Sarah and I were here at 11:30 … We just got to talking and I lost track of time."

"You know the rules."

As if his voice wasn't bad enough, that gray gaze of his pierced my defenses. Yet he sat so nonchalantly on my bed, dressed only in his navy blue flannel pajama bottoms. For a man in his late-thirties, he was incredibly fit. I'd seen him with his shirt off a few times growing up, but this was the first time I'd had a chance to really look. He had an odd tattoo on the side of his ribcage beneath his left armpit. It looked like writing, but I wasn't close enough to read it.

I hated the disappointed scowl on his beautiful face. It brought back too many memories of my accidental misbehaviors as a child. But when I was seven I could always wipe that look from his face by giving him a big hug, a sloppy little-girl kiss on the cheek, and saying how sorry I was. I didn't think that would work now that I was eighteen.

"So, am I grounded?"

"No, baby girl. I think you're a little old for grounding. Drop your pants and bend over my knees."

What? The word shot through my head, unarticulated, but it took me a few more seconds with my mouth hanging open in surprise to actually say out loud.

"What?"

My stepdad's scowl deepened, but it only made him more brutally handsome. The man had chiseled features with angles layered upon angles, and a severe, military haircut that left just enough dark length so that he didn't look entirely bald. His eyes had always been my favorite thing about him, so sweet and kind, but tonight they blazed with anger so dangerous I was a little frightened.

"You broke the rules, baby girl. If you don't want all your privileges revoked for the next three months, *drop trou and bend over.* You never did anything bad enough as a little girl that required a spanking, but I'll be damned if I let you get away with this without some repercussions."

I was too astounded to respond. I stared at him, mouth agape, just trying to find words. Finally I said, "You want to … *spank* me?"

He was suddenly on his feet, looming over me, terrifying in his magnificence. "You will be punished, Case. One way or the other. It's your choice. My hand on your backside, or yes, you're grounded for three months."

My mind spun. Three months of being treated like a fucking child didn't appeal to me at all. It was the beginning of the summer after graduation. I'd be away from my parents soon enough, sure, ensconced in a dormitory at college a few hours away. But I had plans for the summer that would be totally screwed if I had to rely on Sarah for transportation on a daily basis. I had my own car, too, but "grounded" meant driving privileges being revoked as well as the freedom to even leave the house unless I was running errands for my parents.

I scowled back at my stepdad as fiercely as I could.

"Fine. You want to fucking spank me, have at it, you old bastard." I tore the button of my jeans open and threw down the zipper, shoving the denim and my panties down my thighs. I rejoiced at the brief shock on his face when the word "old" sprang from my mouth. I didn't think of him that way, but the bite was meant to hurt. He'd have a few more shocks to deal with if he caught sight of my tattoos. At least the piercings were in places he'd never see.

He gritted his teeth and grabbed my forearm, pulling me across his lap.

"You're a mouthy bitch, aren't you? I don't think I like the way you turned out, Case. I just hope I can instill a little discipline in you before you start to think you know more than the real grown ups. If you can't be a sweet girl anymore, you'll at least learn to follow the rules."

CHAPTER TWO

*T*he air hit my ass a split second before his large palm smacked into my flesh with a loud *thwack*. I cried out, more from surprise than pain. With one hand I inadvertently grabbed his flannel-covered calf to steady myself, and braced the other on the edge of the bed.

"That's just one. You're getting a lot more before I'm done."

My left ass cheek burned from the sharp heat of the strike. The pain subsided quickly, though, simply leaving behind a hot tingle, sinking into my flesh. The tingling part I liked, and I especially liked the buzz of sensation that went deeper, but before I could contemplate enjoying the ordeal, his hand connected hard with my right cheek.

SMACK

Then he hit both at once and sharp, burning stings

bloomed across my ass. The deeper heat grew, confusing me with its insistence. It was the opposite of painful, but the sharp pain that accompanied his relentless slaps confused me.

My pulse was beyond salvaging. My heart raced, both due to the humiliation and the pain. He kept going, barely giving me time to recover between each strike. Tears streamed down my face and I just wished for it to be done so I could be alone and figure out what the hell my body had done to betray me, because I really, really liked it.

I still hated the implication, in spite of it all. It was bad enough that I'd come so close to fucking up my summer break, but to have to endure my stepfather's wrath this way—to be so acutely aware of his disappointment—broke my heart. The knot of emotion in my belly finally burst on about the fifteenth smack of his hot palm on my sore butt.

The sobs came out, unchecked. "I'm sorry, Daddy. I'm so, so sorry." I choked on a sob before I could say more.

His posture shifted and rather than strike my ass again, he stopped, leaving his hand resting lightly atop my lower back on the tail of my shirt, just above the twin infernos that were my ass cheeks.

"What are you sorry for, Casey?" he asked in a low, soft voice.

I drew in a stuttering breath. "For disappointing you. I hate disappointing you. I'm so sorry."

"Not for breaking the rules?"

"I didn't mean to, I promise. Please don't hate me."

"Baby girl, I would never hate you. I just need to make sure you understand there are consequences when you misbehave. Now hold still."

I took a deep breath and buried my face in the bedspread, anticipating more swift punishment, but none came.

The next thing I felt was a cool wetness on my scorched skin, and the scent of lilacs hit my nostrils. I let out an audible sigh as he spread the deliciously chilly lotion over my skin. His fingers were gentle, a sweet contrast to the harsh treatment he'd given me before. They rubbed lightly, smoothing the cream in wide circles over my flesh. It felt just a little too good, with the soft, cool caresses of his fingers on my abused ass. I clenched my eyes shut and held my breath to avoid giving any outward sign that I liked it more than I should. He must have sensed my tension, though.

"Does this feel better?" he asked, his voice strangely deep and gruff. He traced his fingertips along the creased arc beneath one cheek, each slight stroke along my upper thigh sending jolts of pleasure through my over-sensitized skin. He teased perilously close to my core before lifting his hand and doing the same to the other cheek.

I bit back a gasp and did my best to resist wiggling to get more contact.

"It feels nice," I whispered. I wanted to spread my

legs but feared that might give the wrong signal. He was just attending to my abused skin and that was it.

"You're wet," he blurted suddenly. "Did the spanking do this to you?" When he said "this," he did the unthinkable. He pressed his thumb between my thighs and slid it along the crease of my hot folds. I knew I must be sopping wet considering how much my pussy felt like a solid, pulsing knot. It throbbed even more than my ass did, and the contact of his thumb against me didn't help a bit.

I clenched my eyes shut and nodded into the mattress. I was done with this, I decided. There was no way I could take more. He'd spanked me. I said I was sorry. That was enough.

I struggled to stand, but he held me down across his lap with a hand against my shoulder blades.

"Oh no, you don't. I need you to say it out loud, Case. Did my spanking you turn you on?"

Did it turn me on? Did having my hero's bare palm hot against my ass turn me on? Not that I'd ever fantasized about him, except in a very abstract way, but my stepdad embodied everything I found attractive in men. Damn right it turned me on.

Admitting the truth was another issue entirely. But this was my chance. I braced myself and commanded my voice to actually speak.

"Y-yes. And then the lotion. Can I stand up now?"

"No." His palm came down on my ass once again with a loud crack. I yelped and lay still, too overwhelmed with surprise and arousal to form a coherent thought.

My stepdad gripped my ass with both hands and spread my cheeks, murmuring to himself in appreciation. "You are so fucking wet right now. I wonder what I should do about that." His hands slipped over the mounds of my ass and gripped my thighs, pushing them apart. One hand slid up my inner thigh and grazed my sensitive pussy again. I winced, hoping he didn't explore too far.

It was bad enough that he insisted on still punishing me, but humiliating me this badly seemed unlike him.

"Daddy, please. I said I was sorry..." I uttered weakly. This was all wrong. His touch on my thigh made no sense. The way that touch made me even wetter made even less sense. And he was about to discover one of my dark secrets if he kept on teasing me. I needed him to stop before he found out, even though I really wanted him to keep going.

No such luck. The slick tease of his fingertips made it deeper. I gasped when he slipped one long digit deep into me and back out, then moved toward my clit. He paused abruptly when he reached it.

The light flick of his finger over the small, curved steel bar that pierced my hood had me on the verge of orgasm. I couldn't help but moan as he probed and gently rubbed.

My life was fucking over now, I was sure of it. I

could say farewell to summer vacation. Except none of that really mattered at the moment. All I wanted was for him to just rub a tiny bit harder so I could get off. I twitched my hips, hoping he'd get the hint. I'd lost the capacity to care that he was my stepdad doing these things to me, too. I just really, really needed to come.

"Please," I whimpered.

"Do you need to come?" His free hand suddenly snagged my chin and made me turn my head to look at him. "Tell me, Case, do you need to come?"

"Oh, God yes, Daddy. Please let me come." I was halfway mortified to even articulate such a thing, but had relinquished control of my entire life in the last ten minutes, ever since that first, soft brush of his thumb over my wet opening.

He gave me an approving smirk. "All right, baby. Just know that when I'm done, you have a little bit of explaining to do."

With that, his fingers rubbed in quick strokes along my clit, pressing the bar of my piercing right onto the spot it was meant to stimulate, as though he knew precisely how to work it. Swift surges of pleasure radiated out, through my lower body and further, until every single inch of me felt like it vibrated with warmth. I cried out and dug my nails into the free arm he'd used to cradle my shoulders while his other hand did its job on my pussy.

I felt him shift and lean over me as I lost control, his breath hot in my ear and his lips velvety smooth against my neck. "That's right, baby girl. Give it up to me."

He placed a lingering kiss beneath my ear and gave my clit one last little nudge. Tears still streamed down my cheeks, but from ecstasy rather than despair. The kiss brought out a shuddering sigh. It meant he wasn't angry, at least. I suppose the mind-blowing orgasm he'd just given me might have clued me in on that detail already, though.

"Stand up, Casey," he said softly, urging me off his lap. As I shifted back, I leaned into him to catch my balance. My hip leaned tighter against him. The unmistakable thickness of his erection pressed against me for a moment before I finally stood, still shaky from the entire experience.

CHAPTER THREE

I wasn't quite ready for his scrutiny, but I stood as still as I could. It reminded me of every morning growing up, when he'd give me a critical look just before school, like the drill sergeant he'd been, in a former life. I didn't think of him that way when I was younger, though. He was just this big, beautiful hero who I wanted desperately to please.

He still was. Except the pleasing part had acquired a different meaning entirely within the moments since I'd come home. Now, it felt the same way I'd felt getting the piercings. Secret, and dangerous. Even worse than the piercings, though. Almost too bad for me to continue. He was my stepdad, on paper. Yet his expression when I stood was distinctly less than paternal. He looked at me like a drill sergeant looks at a soldier who'd mouthed off. It was so close to how he'd

look when I was little, but there was a distinct differ-
ence now.

When I was little, he'd make a play of it, straight-
ening my clothes, then chucking me under the chin
and kissing me on the forehead before I caught the
school bus. "You're always ship shape, Casey," he said.
"Keep up the good work, sailor."

Now, he looked ready to punish me for something.
Anything. It made me even shakier because I would
take it if he felt I deserved it, even though I knew it
was all a game, like it was years ago. Just a more
grown-up version now.

"Did I do good?" I asked when I finally found my
legs again.

He looked up at me and nodded. "You took it like a
champ, baby. But we're not done yet. I need to know
more about this piercing of yours."

I flinched back involuntarily when he reached out
to tap a finger against the tiny silver orb that adorned
the top of my clit. Even his small contact sent a thrill
straight to my core. I had to close my eyes and take a
slow, deep breath to keep my senses.

"What about it?"

"When did you get this? You're barely eighteen. I
know that might not matter, if you have a fake ID. I
had one at sixteen. I was a crazy kid ..."

"On my birthday," I said, cutting him off.

"Oh? Is it the only one?"

I could have left him then. Just walked out. But he

was in *my room.* I could go lock myself into my parents' room and hide. In his room. Yet this moment seemed too perfect to let go. I'd never been this intimate with Max. My stepdad. My hero. I wanted more. It was no longer enough to have the validation of his approval. His slow questions made my heart beat ever faster. Even though he'd just made me come, I wanted his hands on me again. I wanted the complete surrender that I'd given him in that moment when I'd given it up to him with his finger on my clit.

"No. I have a few more," I said. It was meant to be a challenge, but my voice was still so shaky it came out sounding more like a confession.

"Show me," he said.

It felt like a game now. He wanted me to show myself to him, so I unbuttoned my shirt, sure he'd be livid at what he discovered once I displayed myself. I paused halfway, though. Not quite ready. I caught my breath.

"Casey, you don't have to be afraid," he said. His voice was so soft. It was the voice he used when I was a kid and afraid of monsters in my closet.

"I am afraid of you, you know."

"What? Why?"

The tears welled up again. How the hell did I even express the way I felt? The constant need I had for his approval.

"I'm afraid if I show you, you'll hate me," I managed to snuffle out.

His dark brows creased and he rested both hands on my naked hips. His thumbs swept in soft arcs over my skin, making me wish he was touching me in other spots.

"I will never hate you, Casey. I signed on to love you when I married your mother. Don't you remember the ring I gave you when I proposed to Tanya?"

I did remember. In fact that moment was the day I think I'd first fallen in love with Max, even though I was only six. I'd probably been in love with him for most of my life since that moment. Yet I'd never been so terrified that I'd lose his love until now. What would he think if he saw the rest of me?

I hesitantly opened my blouse and let it slide to the floor, then unclasped my bra at my back. I watched his face the entire time. He seemed to brace himself, his fingers gripping tighter at my hips, when I let the lacy bra fall to the floor and stood fully naked in front of him.

"Christ," he whispered. He lifted a hand off my hip and with a gentle stroke traced the tattoo that adorned my ribcage just below my left breast. When he reached the top of the dark inkwork of the dragon, he hooked the tip of his finger through the hoop that pierced my left nipple. The tugging sensation incited fresh pleasure in my core, and I gasped.

"Why did you do this to yourself, baby? You were so perfect without all this hardware and ink."

"Because it felt good," I said, deciding to be completely honest. "I loved the pain when I got them. And they feel so good now." *So, so good with you touching them.*

"Don't cry, baby. You're beautiful. Do you have any idea what you can do with these, though?"

"J-just feel good, I guess?" I still remembered my mission when I'd gotten them. Partly it had been asserting my self control now that I was technically an adult. Mostly I'd wanted to feel something intense for the first time in my life. I'd been such a good girl my whole childhood, but growing up with Max as my stepdad had been mesmerizing. He'd been intense, yet I'd never been more than his little girl. Like I was in some kind of bubble that couldn't be sullied by the emotion he seemed to keep to himself. I wanted to feel a little bit of what I thought he felt, with his scars and tattoos.

The tattoo had been the first thing I tried, and the memory of the pain still gave me a rush. After that, I'd had my nipples pierced with twin steel hoops. I couldn't stop there, once it was done. When I asked the tattooist what other options I had that I could hide easily, he'd hedged. When I told him I didn't want my navel pierced because it sounded too cliche, he hesi-tated and then pulled out a binder with photos of women's privates and the dazzling jewelry that was nestled in each unique arrangement of soft, pink flesh.

"I want this," I'd said, pointing at a photo with the

pink hood of a woman's clit, run through with a curved steel bar capped on both ends with little spheres.

I had no other plans after that. The pain was so sweet. It made me feel powerful. Like I could endure anything if I could endure that. What I couldn't endure was Max's disappointment, however.

"No, baby. These are meant for much, much more than simply feeling *good*." He tugged lightly at each of the hoops. "They're meant to make you feel *everything*."

CHAPTER FOUR

*M*y voice hitched when I tried to ask, "Everything?"

"Did you like being spanked? I never did it to you when you were little. You were always a good girl."

"But now I'm bad?"

He smiled. "Yeah, I wouldn't have done this if you weren't. But bad doesn't mean I don't love you. It just means I might have to punish you."

I let out a shaky sigh. "Okay. I'm ready." I wasn't quite sure what he meant by punishment, but I trusted him implicitly.

He rose slowly, his eyes holding mine. "Stay here," he said, and left the room.

I stood there, sniffling for a moment, then sat on the bed. My body still buzzed from his touch. He was going to punish me more, I knew. I probably deserved it for disappointing him. But something shifted inside me, like the tumblers of a lock falling open when the right key pushed inside and turned. He was going to punish me, and I couldn't wait for it.

I dropped a shaky hand between my legs, curious if my body cared as much as my mind did. My fingers met hot flesh and drew back slick fluid. Even anticipating his next move had me hot and eager. But I couldn't encourage it, I knew that much. I'd broken his rules. That's what this was all about, after all. My ass still stung from the spanking but I had a strange hope that he'd do that again. What the hell was he doing now, though?

A moment later, he came back. My heart lept at the sight of him. Then stuttered to a near halt when I caught view of the heavy case he set down on the floor of my bedroom.

And if the case wasn't enough of a shock, he turned and closed the door behind him, then flipped the lock. Who the hell would come? Mom was out of town for eight more days and we didn't regularly have guests unless she was home.

I stared up at Max. He'd changed, too. He wore a pair of snug black leather pants that hugged his muscular legs and ass. Steel glimmered among the tattoos on his chest. I'd seen him shirtless before, so I'd seen the ink, but now … his nipples sported a pair of hoops just like mine and the center of his lower lip had a stud right through it. Both of his earlobes sported silver hoops, too.

"Jesus, Daddy. When did you do all that?"

"A long time ago, baby. I thought I oughta hide it, but I think it's better for you if you see it." His voice remained deep and even. I wanted to ask if Mom knew, but decided bringing her into the conversation would be the wrong move. I lost sight of his beautiful face when he stooped to unlock the case he'd brought in. It was one of those big, split-top cases that opened in the center and had hinges halfway down. I couldn't see what was inside.

When he came back to me he had his hands around a couple large orbs of shining steel.

"These are for you," he said. "A little lesson for disobeying me."

I gripped the bedspread in each hand where they rested by my thighs, trying to conceal my nerves while I leaned forward to inspect my next lesson.

Each orb had a tiny latch attached to it. Before I had a chance to object, he attached one on the hoop that pierced my left nipple, then the other on my right hoop.

"Ahh!" I cried out at the instant pain that shot through me when the weight pulled at my flesh. "Fuck! Take them off!"

He abruptly cupped my breasts, holding the orbs close so the pain stopped.

He leaned into me and murmured in my ear, "No. This is your first lesson, Case. You want to keep these piercings, then you need to learn what they're good for." Then he released my breasts and let the weights dangle again, the pain shooting through me in searing bursts.

"Daddy, this hurts!"

"So make it not hurt."

I reached a hand up to remove one, but he clamped his palm down hard on my wrist.

"No, baby. You're not allowed to touch them."

My nipples were in agony. I needed to make it stop somehow. The weight of the steel balls was too much. I spun around, clutched my breasts for a moment.

"No touching," Max said.,

I dropped my hands to my sides and stared at the pillows on my bed. I had too many pillows, but maybe that was a good thing. I crawled up onto my bed, grabbed a few of my pillows, and shoved them under my aching chest.

I sighed when the pain finally subsided.

"Perfect," I heard from behind me. "You have an amazing ass, Casey. So spankable."

As if to illustrate the point he smacked my ass hard.

"Do you know how to follow rules now, Casey? Because I'm going to give you a few."

"Yes," I said.

"Good. The first rule is that you do what I tell you to do. Do you understand?"

"Yes."

"The second rule is that if you're ever unhappy or in too much pain, you have to tell me no, but we need a word that really, really *means* no. If I'm doing anything that makes you unhappy or uncomfortable you say this word. I'll let you choose it."

"Um … Christmas?" I blurted it out without thinking. I craned my head around to try to see him, but all I could make out was the silhouette of him in his leather pants. I was acutely aware of his hand on my ass, though, still stroking like he hadn't just slapped me again.

"Christmas is good. If you ever want me to stop what I'm doing, just say Christmas. Are you ready?"

Ready for what? My nipples still ached from the heavy balls he'd hung on them. I couldn't even move without causing myself pain. So I just stayed there, ass in the air.

The first smack was beyond the round of spanking he'd given me earlier. My ass rang with pain.

"You are such a bad girl, Case," his deep voice said. "Maybe you'll learn a little from this."

His palm hit my other cheek hard. The pain spread quickly, but the lingering sting and vibrating aftershocks of pleasure only made me hotter. Learn a little? What the fuck would I learn except that my stepdad had a wicked slap that turned me on? Like my experience with the piercings, I suddenly had the urge to test my own limits.

"You've gotta do better than that, Daddy," I said, goading him.

I was rewarded with a sharp smack that resounded through the room.

"You want better, baby? I'll show you better."

I heard him rustling in his case again but held still. I wanted to be surprised.

The swift movement of his hands surprised me when the soft cuffs clicked around my wrists. He made swift work of the scarves tied to my headboard, loosely securing them to the shackles. I could still move, but not much.

Cool fluid hit my ass and I gasped.

"That's lube, sweetheart. I'm going to shove something in your tight little ass in a second. I just wanted you to know."

His hand gripped my ass cheek and squeezed just as the smooth tip of whatever it was pressed against my butthole. It took no effort on his part to slide the object into me. It felt good. Even better than the times I'd tried it myself with my fingers. Cool and smooth and almost nonexistent. At least until I twitched and every nerve in my ass felt it.

"Jesus." I didn't mean to say it out loud but I couldn't help myself.

"You like that?" He asked. The chuckle that followed pissed me off. I liked it too much, but I was increasingly growing jaded about my love for my stepdad.

"I hate it," I said, just to be contrary. "I hate you!"

"All right, maybe you need something bigger in

your ass, but that'll have to happen another day. You remember the rules, right? The word you need to use if you want me to stop?"

"Yes, you fucker. I know how to speak." I gave him my best sulky tone. The one that made him glower at me and verbally reprimand me when I was younger. I hoped it might incite some new pleasurable torture now, though.

He laughed. But all I cared about was what else he'd violate me with. I squeezed the pillows under my chest. I could get up and confront him head on if I wanted to. If I could endure the pain of the weights hooked to my nipples.

I didn't want to, though. I wanted to know how far he would go if I kept pushing him.

"Does your ass hurt, baby?"

"Yeah, you jerk. You spanked me."

The hard strike surprised me when it hit.

"Ow!"

"Oh, now you start crying. You weren't crying when I had my finger on your clit. Did you like that orgasm, Case?"

He smacked my ass again and I clenched reflexively around the plug. A fresh wash of pleasure hummed through me, making my clit throb.

"Tell me if you liked my finger on your sweet little pierced clit, Case. If you ever want to feel me rub that little nub again, tell me."

"Daddy, you're such an asshole!"

"I'm not arguing, but you still have to answer."

"Fine. I loved your finger on my clit, all right?" I loved the fuck out of his finger on my clit now, too, because it was there, just as I made the confession, pressing and toying with the steel rod.

CHAPTER FIVE

"*J*esus, Case. Were you always this responsive?"

I whimpered at the stretching sensation of his fingers sinking into my tight channel. The piercings and ink probably gave him the wrong idea about me. I'd never really had sex before. I just knew I liked the way the needles felt, the rush of the stings on my flesh and the exquisite buzz of adrenaline that lingered after the pain stopped. I bit my lip to avoid crying out. Another of his fingertips rested against my clit and began to rub in a tight circle while he continued fucking into me with two thick digits.

"No," he said, as though he'd made a decision. The touching stopped, much to my dismay. "Jesus I want to fuck you like you couldn't believe. But you need to learn first."

His hand struck my ass hard enough that I cried out. I felt like a fool, though, because I loved it and wanted more. He stepped up closer, resting a leather-clad knee on the bed beside me. His rough, stubbled chin brushed my shoulder and his lips tickled my ear.

"You're mine. This is just a bit of fun to prove it."

His hand landed on my ass again in a hard strike, followed by a circular stroke, then another strike, right over top of the end of the plug. My pussy thrummed with pent-up need.

"Tell me you're mine, Casey," he said, landing the next smack square on my swollen pussy. The sting of the strike on the wet flesh sank deeper, the combination of pleasure and pain making me cry out.

"If you want more, I want you to say it, baby." Another smack, this time quicker and further between my thighs, right over my clit. Warm pleasure bloomed out from the throbbing bundle. Oh, God, I needed him to do that exact thing again.

"I'm yours, Daddy. I'm all yours. Please don't stop."

"If you're mine, then I need you to do something for me. Open your mouth."

I craned my head to look up at him. The angle gave me an amazing view of his sculpted torso, beginning with the prominent ridge of a hard cock inside the dark leather pants. His muscles rippled when he cupped one hand around the stiff bulge, and then slowly unfastened the buttons of the fly.

My heart raced in anticipation. I knew what he wanted, and I wanted so badly to do it right, but I had no idea how. His brow creased when he met my apprehensive gaze, and he paused.

"You can say the word, Case. I won't force you to do anything you don't want."

I nodded. "It's not that. I'm afraid I'll do it wrong. That you won't like it."

He stepped off the bed and crouched down so he was at eye level. His large hand cupped my face, his palm warm and slightly calloused. I leaned into him, grateful for the gentle touch.

"You've never been a disappointment in your entire life," he said. "Tonight just proved how perfect you are. Beyond my wildest dreams."

I nodded and gave him a nervous smile.

"That's my girl," he whispered and leaned in. He pressed his lips softly against mine. I felt him sigh against me just before his tongue darted out, sweeping between my lips. It was as though he was tasting me, but only for an instant before he pulled back.

"Daddy's gonna fuck this pretty mouth now. If you need me to stop, squeeze this." He placed a small object into my cuffed hand. It was a tiny little noise-maker. I squeezed it once, experimentally, and it made a loud clicking noise.

Then he was kneeling on the bed again, his cock thick and hard and aimed at my cheek. I had to turn my head to face it dead on. He had a piercing, too, a steel hoop a little thicker than mine that rested just under the tip. The masculine musk of him pervaded my senses and I opened my mouth wide, inviting him in.

"That's my girl," he murmured. "Lick it, first. Just run your tongue around the tip and tease the hoop."

I did as he asked, darting my tongue out. The salty flavor of him was a shock as much as the absolute velvety softness of his skin. A tiny bead of moisture leaked from his tip and I wrapped my lips around him impulsively, pressing my tongue into the slit.

"Jesus, Case. You might be a natural. Can you take me deeper?"

I nodded, my pulse still racing, but not out of fear now. I could do this. Hell, I loved the taste and feel of him on my tongue.

He clutched the back of my neck, fingers digging in and holding my head steady as he tilted his hips. I opened my mouth wider, relishing the velvet heat of his shaft sliding along my tongue.

"That's right, baby. Oh, fuck. Now suck a little."

I nearly gagged when the steel hoop hit the back of my throat, but controlled the reaction by taking a deep breath through my nose. The angle I had to turn my head to take him became uncomfortable, but his fingers at the back of my neck massaged me as he pressed my head down onto him, lessening the stress on my muscles.

His little words of praise kept me going. Once he seemed to find a rhythm, suddenly his free hand landed hard on my ass. I moaned around his cock, tears springing to my eyes from the sting.

"That's right, you're still a bad girl, but you're redeeming yourself right now. Keep sucking, baby, and I'll keep spanking you."

I made an "mmhmm" noise around the thick column of flesh that filled my mouth.

He spanked me again, then slid his fingers between my legs, teasing between my folds in long swipes, just barely toying at my clit. I made a whimpering sound of dismay, that I hoped he could interpret.

"You want to come again, don't you?" he asked. I responded with an affirmative hum and raised my gaze beseechingly.

He slid his cock out of my mouth and stood, his leather pants halfway hanging off his narrow hips and snagged on the thick curves of his muscular thighs. I swallowed, sure my face looked a mess from the saliva that had escaped my mouth while I sucked him.

"You've earned it, then. Let's just make sure you can enjoy it, all right?"

He reached beneath me and I felt gentle tugs at each of my breasts as he removed the heavy weights from my nipples. Then he removed the cuffs that secured my wrists to the headboard.

"Don't move. I want you just like this, but I need you to be able to move, that's all."

He stripped out of his pants and disappeared from my field of view. The bed dipped down behind me and a moment later his hot thighs rubbed against mine, the hairs of his legs tickling my bare skin. He smacked his cock in a swift series of strikes against the crease of my ass, right on top of the plug, then slid the tip down between my lips.

I wondered if it would hurt, the first time. I'd masturbated plenty, so it wasn't like I was going to bleed, but nothing that big had ever been inside me before. I should tell him, I realized.

His hand gripped my hip and the head of his cock was just barely pressed against my opening when I chickened out.

"Christmas!" I blurted, feeling supremely silly, after all we'd done.

He stopped, and pulled back, but didn't move, otherwise.

"What is it, baby?"

"I … I need you to know you're my first, all right? That's all."

He sighed and I felt even greater distance between us. Hesitantly, I looked over my shoulder. He'd fallen back on his haunches, his hands limp at his sides.

"Jesus, Casey. How the hell do you end up pierced to the heavens and not have had sex?"

"I don't know … I just know what I like. Normal sex just seemed too boring for a first time. Daddy, I don't want you to stop. Please! I just needed you to know."

His hand rested comfortingly on my bare ass, fingers stroking. "If I do this, it's a lot more serious. Do you realize that? You're so important to me, Casey. And Jesus Christ, you have always amazed me. Tonight …"

"Beyond your wildest dreams?" I said softly, feeling my heart flutter at the obvious affection and awe in his voice.

"I'm going to make you come so hard, you'll never want another man's cock. I meant it when I said you were mine. Now I know how true that really is."

"I'm ready, Daddy."

He shifted up close to me again and I closed my eyes, waiting.

"God, baby, your pussy is still so wet," he murmured, his fingers sliding between my lips again. "You let me know if it hurts."

"I hope it does," I said. "I never want to forget it."

His hot tip slipped between my folds, spreading me wide. It didn't hurt at first, and I was a little disappointed. Then he pushed deeper and his girth stretched me even more. I let out a harsh gasp and he slowed, his hand rubbing in a comforting swirl on my lower back.

"Just take a deep breath."

"I'm okay. Please don't stop!"

He pushed deeper and I whimpered, but not from

pain. The hard steel of his piercing had hit a tender spot inside me that made my clit pulse wildly. He paused there, seeming to test the depth.

"Does this feel good?" he asked, his voice low and rough. "Because it feels incredible to me."

"Uh huh," I managed to gasp out.

"Jesus, I need to fuck you hard. Your pussy is so goddamn tight and hot."

"So fuck me."

With that, he rammed in deep enough that I saw stars. I clenched the pillows and cried out. He didn't move again for several moments. When I finally caught my breath I felt his body bend over mine, his strong arms wrapping around me. The pressure of his pelvis pushed the plug deeper into my ass. I had a split second to wonder at the dismissal of that little object, but didn't care now that he was inside me.

"That's the hard part, baby. The rest is slow and wonderful. Come here."

I was beyond objecting, even if I could find words for it. He filled me up in a way I couldn't even imagine.

He pulled me upright against him, his thighs supporting mine and my back against his muscled chest. His hands cupped both my breasts so delicately, his thumbs brushing as light as feathers over my still-sore nipples. The light contact made me shudder as much as his breath in my ear as he began to fuck me in earnest.

"You are amazing, Case. Next time, I know you'll astound me again."

Next time, he said. I smiled to myself, already imagining what kinds of pleasure "next time" would hold in store, even as he blew my mind with pleasure in the current moment.

CHAPTER SIX

*M*y body ached deliciously when I woke up to late morning sun streaming through my windows the next morning. I remembered dissolving into tears after having another mind-blowing orgasm and feeling Dad's cock pulsing in me. The sensations had been overwhelming in so many ways. He'd stayed and held me until I passed out from sheer exhaustion.

I felt amazing now, though, in spite of the soreness. I tested every muscle, particularly the ones that had gotten the roughest workouts. My pussy tingled pleasantly. My ass was a tiny bit sore, but it was a good kind of sore. I looked forward to finding out what else he would do with it, next time. When would next time be?

Noises drifted up from downstairs, along with the delicious smell of breakfast. My stomach grumbled. I dragged myself out of bed, enjoying the way the soft sheets slid over my naked skin and remembering the soft caresses of his hands touching me everywhere.

When I came out of my bathroom, freshly showered, I stopped cold. On the armchair by the window was a note and an assortment of items that hadn't been there before.

I picked up the note and read.

"You will wear this today, all day. And if I ask you to bend over, you will do so. When you come down to breakfast you will also have the vibrator securely positioned inside that pretty, tight snatch of yours. You are MY breakfast, Casey, and I want you hot and fresh. *If you don't follow the rules, you will get another spanking.*"

Draped over the chair was a pretty, filmy white negligee with pink flowers on the bodice, and a pair of matching panties. Nestled on the panties was a silver egg-shaped object, with a looped cord at one end.

Breakfast was going to be very interesting, that's for sure. I just had to decide which rule I should break next.Book Two

PART II
DISCOVERY

*ou will wear this today, all day. And if I ask
you to bend over, you will do so. When you
come down to breakfast you will also have the
vibrator secure inside that pretty, tight snatch of yours. You
are MY breakfast, Casey, and I want you hot and fresh."*

The words seemed alien to me at first and it took
me a couple passes to grasp their meaning. I stared
down at the gauzy confections of undergarments Max
had laid out for me. I was eager to wear them, but the
tiny little egg-shaped object that nestled on top of the
sheer, lacy garments might be too much.

I put off thinking about the egg for now, and after
donning a negligee that pushed my boobs up allur-
ingly I had the urge to pick it up.

The egg felt cool in my palm. So serene, and all I
had to do was push it inside my pussy. Then go down
to breakfast with *him*.

He wants me. Max wanted *me.* The events of the night before ran through my mind again. Every moment from the first smack of his hand on my bare backside to his discovery of all my dirty little secrets. I'd lain in his arms afterward, asking him question after question about what the old Max had been like, before meeting my mother and settling down. I'd been a little in love with him my entire life in that abstract way little girls have of idolizing father figures, but until last night never realized how much alike we were now that I was a woman.

Something about him had seemed sad, though, and he hadn't stayed. "You should sleep, Case. I'll see you in the morning." And he left, turning out the light but leaving the door slightly open like he'd always done when I was younger and afraid of the dark. I'd lain awake in the dark, perplexed by his mood and aching a little to understand him enough to comfort him. Perhaps this morning I could get him to open up some more.

That was enough to get me moving. The slinky garment was incredibly revealing and I loved it. It draped over my curves and pushed my breasts up. It left my nipples bare, but I liked that part, too. I tweaked and teased at them both, tugging lightly on my hoops just until the sting sent my core aching again like it had under Max's attention. Then I revisited the idea of the egg. It had a neat little loop at one end, which I guessed was to help get it out after …

after what? I couldn't find an on switch. It was just a solid little oblong shape, with the slightest seam in it that I guessed was how to replace the batteries. I wasn't so naive that I didn't know it was a vibrator, but it was perplexing.

I pressed the tapered end between my slick labia and sighed in pleasure as it slid in easily. It wasn't anywhere near as large as Max's beautiful cock, but it still left me feeling a tiny bit of pressure in a very nice spot. I took a few steps across the room, worried at first that it might slip out, but it stayed securely seated inside me. I picked up the panties and started to put them on, but paused, thinking how much I wanted Max's hands on my bare backside again, punishing me for disobeying him.

My head buzzed with the tiny rebellion as I let the small bit of lacy fabric fall back to the chair and I stood and went to the door.

My pulse pounded in my ears on the way into the hallway. Our house seemed too small for me suddenly, too quaint and perfect for the unusual turn my life had taken in just the last twenty-four hours. The sexy lingerie I wore felt right, but the walls that surrounded me seemed to close in, leaving me with an uncomfortable itch. The carpeted staircase didn't fit right, either, nor did the flowery decor of the family room. It wasn't until I followed the sound of Max's low voice into the kitchen and saw him standing quietly beside the breakfast table, facing away from me, that I felt like I was truly in the right place.

He wore the same leather pants he'd donned the night before, but was otherwise naked and barefoot. His inked upper arms and shoulders rippled with tension as he gripped the phone in his hand. I stood quietly just outside the doorway, goosebumps prickling my skin while I waited for him to notice me.

"… I'm not going to fucking draw this out now, man. It's way too late. The papers came yesterday and she called this morning to make sure I signed, so it's done. Bring your tiedowns. There's just one thing I need to handle before you get here—I made a big mistake last night. Nah, I'll talk about it after we get this shit handled. Thanks. See you in a few."

He ended the call and set the phone down, leaning into the counter with his head bowed. He'd made a mistake? That couldn't have meant me. I really, really hoped it didn't mean what had happened. Not after the way we'd talked in the dark before he left my bed. A low chill gathered in my belly, regardless.

While I watched unnoticed from the doorway he reached across the counter and gripped a sheaf of papers in his hand, stared at them for a second, then tossed them down again with a curse. His knuckles whitened when he gripped a ballpoint pen and stabbed the tip to the bottom edge of one sheet and scribbled something there, then shoved everything aside.

He turned, then, and stopped cold when his eyes landed on me.

"Holy shit, Casey," he bit out, scowling for a split second. His eyes swept over me and his expression softened, his gaze growing heated. "Christ," he said, licking his lips and letting his look linger over my bare breasts.

"This is what you wanted, isn't it?"

"I …" he faltered and swallowed. "Yeah, baby. You look …" He sighed deeply and shook his head, his reaction causing my own eager anticipation to deflate. "Listen. I made a mistake last night. We shouldn't have done what we did, but I was … Fuck, there's no excuse for it. I'm sorry."

"No …" I turned my head slowly back and forth to try to suppress the humiliation that sent a chill washing through me beginning with a tingling sensation at the top of my scalp. "Tell me why. Did you have second thoughts because of Mom?"

It was the first time I'd even thought about my mother since I'd come home the night before. She was gone so often and we barely got along as it was when she was home. It would have been kind to say that I resented her and the fact that she had him. I resented her even more now.

"Not exactly," he said. "Well, indirectly maybe. Just go back upstairs and get dressed. We can talk about it after. *Please*."

A raw sensation clutched at my belly and the cold

flood of humiliation was replaced by hot anger. "Fuck that," I said. "Do you expect me to just forget what happened? The things you showed me … You can't just expect me to stop now. I don't care why I got so lucky, but I have to know why you won't give me more."

"Your mother's divorcing me, Case." He picked up the papers he'd been looking at and waved them in the air. "I got these yesterday while you were out. Last night happened because of my messed up judgment. I was pissed and hurt and decided to take it out on you in a way I shouldn't have — I saw it as getting back at her, but it got out of control. Jesus, do you have any idea how *wrong* it was?"

"I loved it," I said softly.

He winced. "You're just a kid. You don't know any better."

"I'm eighteen and I know enough to know Mom doesn't deserve you. I don't think she ever really understood you, did she? I just know that I've never really understood myself so well as I did last night with you. I thought these cravings I had made me a freak, but you made everything make sense. Daddy … *Max* … if you don't show me what you know, I'll learn about it some other way. I have to know more. I have to know everything."

I hated myself a little for the pleading. It wasn't something I liked to do, but after a taste of what Max could offer, I wasn't ready to let it end yet.

"Baby, I hear you. Just get dressed, okay? Rick will

be here any second. I don't want him to see you like that."

"What if I want him to see me?" I raised my chin higher and pushed my shoulders back, making my breasts stick out more. "Maybe he can teach me what you won't. I bet the knows your secrets, doesn't he? That would make two of us."

"Fucking hell, Casey," he growled as he stormed past me into the living room and up the stairs. At the same moment a shadow darkened the back door. A heavy knock sounded just before the door swung open and Rick's sturdy, fit frame stepped in, clad in jeans, a dark t-shirt, and work boots.

CHAPTER EIGHT

*R*ick and Max had always been tight and I'd envied their relationship. My friendship with Sarah was coming close to the kind of loyalty I saw between my stepdad and his best friend, but I had a feeling you had to go to war with someone before you could find the kind of unspoken understanding the pair of them had.

Not to mention during family barbecues the pair were always the best looking men at the party. Where my stepdad was dark haired, Rick was a blond Adonis, with curly hair he'd let grow since the military. He was also one of the sweetest men I'd ever met, always bringing gifts for me or my mother, which made it all the more tragic when his wife had been killed a few years earlier. He hadn't been the same since.

Rick's greeting died on his lips when he caught sight of me.

I gave him a little wave. "Heya, Rick. Fancy seeing you here," I said in a cheery tone.

Blue eyes wide with shock, he gaped at me. His tanned and blond-stubbled face went slack with surprise. He stared at me for several moments, then scrubbed his palms over his face and shook his head as though he still didn't believe what he saw.

"Casey … I—I'm sorry … fuck. I should probably go."

"Wait," I said, and he paused before opening the door again to escape. "I have a question for you."

He cleared his throat and kept his gaze deliberately averted from me, though his jeans looked uncomfortably tight just in front. He nodded, "Ah, sure, what is it?"

"You've known Max a long time, right? Did you ever notice anything unusual about his, um, sexual preferences?" I scrunched up my face when I said the words, going for subtle but hoping he'd get the hint, especially if he knew the kinds of details I hoped he did.

Heavy footsteps thunked down the stairs. Behind me Max said, "Don't answer that, you'll only encourage her."

A heavy terrycloth robe draped over my shoulders, but I shrugged it off.

Rick studied his boots thoughtfully for a moment, then turned and leaned his shoulder against the door. He looked at Max where he stood beside me, holding the robe again and looking like he was about to wrap me in it like a straitjacket.

"Since when are you 'Max' to her, buddy?" Rick chuckled and looked at me again, making a low mm-mm sound in his throat. "Big mistake doesn't even come close if this is what you meant. If you were hoping to get even with Tanya, I think you went a little overboard."

I sidestepped Max and sauntered a few steps closer to Rick. "You'd be contributing to my education if you answer my question, Rick. Tell my *stepfather* that he can't close the door now that he's flung it wide open." I turned to look back at Max, my heart pounding in my chest over the exhilaration of my rebellion — something I'd never really considered doing in my life, in spite of my growing understanding that I wanted something very different than what most girls my age seemed to enjoy — something that wasn't as far out of my reach as I'd thought. "I have no regrets. I hope you don't, either."

Max's shoulders sagged. Rick was grinning from ear to ear and looked almost on the verge of laughter. I might have been offended at his attitude if it hadn't been for the giant hard-on filling the front of his jeans.

"I think I need a quick rundown of exactly what you did, Max," he said. "Just so I can make an informed decision about what I should or shouldn't tell the woman." He paused and looked me up and down appraisingly. The frank appreciation in his gaze made my nipples prickle. In a low voice he added, "Because, *my God*, but you are a far cry from a girl now, honey."

I smiled, gratified by his response, and crossed my arms beneath my breasts trying not to betray how breathless I was with the excitement of the moment. I stared at Max with my eyebrows raised. "I'll tell him my version if you want," I said. "I especially liked the part where you …"

"Fuck, all right!" Max yelled. He sat heavily on a bar stool by the kitchen island. "Last night I wasn't exactly in a good place. When you came home I was furious at your mother — twelve years *wasted*. I left behind a life I didn't think I'd ever miss when I married her. The spanking was just my misplaced way to get back at her, but then … goddamn, Casey if I'd known …"

Rick watched us both, his interest never wavering. He glanced at me now.

"What he means is that if he'd known how much I'd enjoy being spanked, maybe he wouldn't have done it. Isn't that right?"

"Things went a direction they shouldn't have, Casey," Max said.

"Forgive me for calling your bullshit," I said. "You loved it as much as I did."

Rick cleared his throat. "So, what happened next?"

I started to speak, but he raised a hand to stop me. "No, I want to hear it from Max," he said with a serious look.

My stepfather stared down at his hands, flexing his fingers into tight fists and then opening them again. He let out a heavy sigh. "It brought me back to before, man. The heat of her ass under my palm. Goddamn it felt so good, and then I realized she was ..." I bit my lip at the memory of his hand brushing my pussy and discovering how turned on I was, then finding my piercing.

I knew when Max looked at me that he was picturing it as vividly as I was. "She was so wet from it. You know how fucking much I *love* seeing a woman turned on by pain. That was when I think I lost it. Then to find out all the things she'd already done to her body. All but one thing." His voice grew low and soft. "I had to have you, Case. And it had to be like that once I knew that I'd be your first. But I can't let anything else happen ... your mom ..."

Rick and I both erupted with objections at the same time. In the middle of me trying to say, "You don't owe Mom a fucking thing," I heard Rick's words and I stopped and stared at him.

"What did you say?" Max and I both asked.

CHAPTER NINE

"I said, if you don't, *I will*. You know damn well what kind of dangerous shit she could get involved in left to her own devices. Don't forget what happened to Aurora after she left the club. We failed her. Don't let the same thing happen to Casey."

"Aurora and Casey are nothing alike. Aurora's judgment was flawed to begin with."

"She got a bad start and we had the chance to help get her on the right track without hurting herself. We should never have let her leave, and you know that. I'm serious, man." He gestured at me and continued. "Casey's … Well fuck, I know saying this makes it sound supremely creepy, but I love her like a daughter, too. But the fact is, *she isn't your daughter*. She won't even be your stepdaughter in a matter of weeks. What she is, is a gorgeous, young, and *very* determined woman and she needs your guidance."

I stood quiet, though I had to restrain myself from running to Rick and kissing him for such a profound argument. My stepdad's attitude was visibly changing — I could see it in his expression as he worked through everything Rick had said. He eyed me with a level of affection that was more of a comfort than anything. I'd never doubted that he loved me, but his look made me feel a little guilty for asking him to do this thing for me ... to show me how to be like him. Rick clearly knew precisely what that meant, though.

"How do you know so much about ... all this?" I asked, looking at Rick. "Who— who is Aurora?"

He looked a little wistful at first. "Max and I have always been a team. In the Navy and then after. We were pros at *all this* once upon a time. Under a Domme named Chloe." He looked a Max. "Those were the days, huh? We could have it again if we wanted, now that we're both about to be unattached."

"Don't fucking remind me," Max said, frowning and glancing with venom at the sheaf of papers on the counter.

Ignoring him, Rick continued. "Aurora was a woman — not much older than you — who we took under our wing. Things didn't go too well with her, though."

"She could never follow the rules," Max said. "It wasn't just about pleasure, Casey. It was also a job for us. There are right ways and wrong ways to approach the lifestyle and she had all the wrong ideas. We tried …"

"But we couldn't turn her around," Rick finished. "She left and sort of dropped off the map for awhile. When we found her again we were way too late."

"What happened to her?" I asked, instinctively covering my breasts in light of the serious turn the conversation had taken. A draft came through from the screen door and blew up my nighty at the same time, completely contradicting my urge for modesty.

Rick's eyes flicked to my exposed, naked hips and his eyebrows twitched. He blinked a couple times and coughed. "Uh … um, institutionalized. Bipolar disorder apparently, probably not much we could have done to help that, but she'd obviously been abused since we'd seen her."

"She hooked up with a sketchy Dom after she left us," Max said. "Not someone who was sanctioned by Chloe's club. We know others, though, Case. I'm not going to just let you figure this out on your own. There's the right Dom out there for you. I'll help you find one."

Rick made a low noise in his throat, probably in response to the angry look I shot at Max.

"I don't want someone else. I want you. Or … or Rick. I trust both of you."

"That part was obvious," Rick said with a grin. "I can't imagine you'd hang out half naked in a room with two men you didn't trust."

Max shot Rick a glare and was rewarded with a helpless shrug. He remained silent, deliberating. I hated this part because it usually meant I'd end up having to make some stupid compromise at the end.

"All right," Max said, standing again. He crossed his arms and gave me an almost stern look. If I hadn't seen the corners of his mouth twitch, I might have taken the look seriously. As it was, he looked like he was about to start a game that he knew he would win, but Max had always been more about playing the game.

"Really?" I asked, smiling broadly.

"As long as I have help, if that's all right with the two of you. I'd be more comfortable if Rick was involved. To keep me honest." He dropped his arms and stepped toward me. "If we're going to do this, baby, we're doing it right, but I won't lie to you. You mean the world to me. I got carried away last night and I can't let that happen again."

I gazed up at him, entranced by the intensity in his eyes. He raised a hand and brushed a knuckle lightly down my cheek. My eyelids fluttered closed in response to the sensation and I let out a slow exhalation when his thumb caressed my lower lip.

Warm skin grazed against the front of my body as he shifted his hand to the back of my neck and pulled me close. His mouth descended to mine, his tongue warm and wet between my lips. I opened up to him with a small moan. God, how much I wanted this. More of what I'd only had a taste of so far.

Rick's throat cleared and his hand rested on the bare skin of my shoulders from behind. "Remember why we're here, man," Rick said.

Max pulled away with a tiny sound of regret. "Yeah. We have work to do, don't we Casey? You need to learn how to follow the rules, first of all. I think you forgot something when you got dressed this morning."

His hands slid down my back, caressing gently over the round contour of my ass. One hand shoved the hem of my nighty up and abruptly he lifted the other hand and brought it down in a loud *smack* against my flesh. I jumped and squeaked in response, clutching at his sides with my fingernails.

He held me against his chest with his other arm, and did it again. The broad, warm flesh of his palm met my ass with a sharp crack. I gasped, the bright burn of pain flooding through me, heating my core and spreading through my body like wildfire.

"That's right, Baby. You misbehave, you get punished." *Smack.*

I bit into his chest when his hand struck me again, and again, the burn stinging more and more each time. And each time he struck me, the force pushed my hips against him until I was as acutely aware of the steel-like ridge of his cock pressing against my belly.

I loved that he loved doing this to me as much as I loved having it done, but I wanted so much more. I turned my face so that my cheek rested against his chest. Max paused for a moment, his hand lightly clutching my sore bottom.

Rick was standing to the side, simply watching, alert.

"You brought ropes for loading the truck, right?" Max asked. "Think they're good enough to re-purpose temporarily?"

Rick laughed. "Yeah, you're not going to believe this … be right back."

He disappeared out the door and I sighed into Max's chest. "Thank you," I said sincerely. Tension had built up all morning and for the first time since I'd come downstairs, I felt like all was right in the world again.

"Don't thank me yet. We're only getting started. One thing you need to learn is to pace yourself, all right? If you *ever* have doubts about continuing, even if it's just a physical limitation, you say so."

I nodded into his chest, inhaling the scent of his aftershave that had acquired a completely new and wonderful association for me in the past twenty-four hours.

His hand clutched my chin and urged me to look at him. "I need you to say you understand, Case. I'm not fucking around here."

"I understand," I said. I cast a quick glance at Rick who had just come back in with a handful of neatly wrapped bundles of white rope.

Max caught sight of what Rick held and laughed. "That's not exactly what I'd call tiedown rope, man … Why the hell would you waste good silk ropes to help me move?"

"It's what I had on hand. I wasn't exactly using the stuff. Thought it should go to some use and I'm glad I brought it now. Must be fate, huh?" He grinned.

Max nodded and looked down at me again with a sparkle in his eyes. "I have a feeling you might be right. Bend over the table now, Casey." He moved the chairs aside and nodded toward the small breakfast table that could seat four. I swallowed and stepped over to it, then leaned forward, placing my palms flat against the cool glass surface. \

*M*ax gripped my shoulder and his mouth was at my ear again. "I asked you to bend over," he said, sliding his palm lower pushing gently against the center of my back.

I bent at the waist and elbows, lowering my torso until my breasts pressed against the glass, the steel hoops in my nipples clinking softly. The tightness of them sent thrills through the tips of my breasts and my pussy clenched tightly around the vibrator, which I'd forgotten until that moment, but with the shift of my pelvis was now a very obvious presence inside me.

I turned my head and rested my hot cheek against the cool surface of the table, darting my eyes around in an effort to see where my stepfather was. I couldn't see him, but I heard him behind me somewhere. A second later I heard a whistling sound and something thin and hard smacked against he lower curves of my ass cheeks. I yelped loudly, the sharp sting bringing water to my eyes. He wasn't using his hand this time.

"It stings a bit when you misbehave, doesn't it, Casey?" he said. The whistle sounded again and I braced myself. The stinging smack hit a little higher that time and I cried out again. My hands shot to the curved edge of the table and clutched tightly at it. I was determined not to move or cry, even though the whipping fucking *hurt* this time. It wasn't anything like the broad smacks of his hand, and it left behind a much deeper burn that tingled all the way to my clenching pussy. I found myself craving another stroke just so I could be sure that's what it was that made my entire body feel alive with excitement.

Suddenly the egg inside me buzzed to life and my hips jerked at the abrupt sensation of pleasure that gripped my lower body. My knuckles grew white from my grip on the edge of the table. The vibration was too intense and right against that sensitive spot inside me that Max had so expertly discovered last night with his cock. The buzzing stopped and I took a breath, but just as I was about to relax, the vibrations started again, followed by another swift, stinging stroke of the switch. A soft sob escaped my throat, partly from the pleasure, and partly from the pain. Max paused again for the span of a breath, leaving my body still and unassaulted both internally and externally.

I braced myself for the strike and the vibration, and

they came in tandem again, multiples in quick succession. Overwhelmed by the sensations that claimed my body, my mind grew hazy, every ounce of my attention focused on my throbbing core and the molten heat of sensations that spread through me. Just when I believed I couldn't possibly feel any more aroused another sensation joined everything else. Cool wetness touched my ass, alien and shocking in contrast to the heat of the whipping and the ache in my pussy. A tiny part of my brain managed to interpret it as lube, but only when the rounded tip of the steel plug pressed against my tight little hole. I clenched reflexively, gasping at the unexpected invasion.

Rick's jeans-clad hips slipped into my field of vision and he squatted down. "Relax, honey. It won't hurt." His gaze moved down my side, his blue eyes fixed on Max's steady, slow probing with the tip of the plug. "It's not quite as big as it feels."

"It feels huge," I said, laughing.

Rick reached out an arm and the press disappeared from my ass. His hand came into view again and he held up the gleaming object. I'd seen the one Max had used on me the night before, and this one was slightly bigger. It was about the length of my thumb and teardrop-shaped, but no thicker at it's widest end than Max's cock.

"Is it … it's to stretch me so you can fuck me, right?" I asked.

"Mostly it's just to give you a new sensation, but yeah … your ass needs some prep before it gets fucked, if that's what you want to happen. Do you like the way it feels?" he asked.

I nodded and started to say exactly how much I liked it, but my words flitted from my mind when a light, warm touch brushed down over the sensitive, slick flesh between my cheeks. Max's fingertip made a slow circuit just around my clenched opening and then pressed.

"This is just my finger, baby. Do you like this?"

"Oh, God, yeah."

"Do you think you can take the plug? I need to do other things with my hands."

Like spank me, I thought, a little giddy over all the different options I had. Rick and Max were the ones with all the experience, and I had so very little. I wanted to know everything, though. Max hadn't said I couldn't ask, either.

"First I want …" I hesitated, biting my lip and staring at Rick's tan face, embarrassed for the first time about what I wanted to ask.

"What is it?" he asked.

I almost couldn't get the words out, as distracted as I was with Max's finger teasing me.

"I want to see you," I said. "See if you're bigger than … *that*." I shifted my eyes to the plug.

"All right," he said and stood. "Hold onto this for a sec, will you?" He placed the shining object in my hand

and I held it, surprised for a second by its weight and how warm it was after being held in Rick's grip.

He tugged his t-shirt over his head while I watched and his tan, tattooed muscles rippled as he stretched. He sat again, taking his time to unlace and pull off his work boots and socks, mostly keeping his eyes on mine while he did so, though he seemed to share what looked like a meaningful glance with Max every few seconds.

The light teasing of my ass didn't stop and I found myself reflexively tilting my hips to meet Max's touch. The first time his finger slid deeper I let out a breath of surprise, but didn't jerk away. The friction felt so nice, just beyond the tight barrier.

Rick slid his jeans off his hips and I swallowed thickly, eyeing his hips and the gorgeous, long cock. His shaft jutted from the trimmed gold thatch between his thighs. He was shaped different than Max, his length a little less thick but no less beautiful. He curved upward slightly and was a little bit longer, without any piercings, but with Max's slow stroking of me from the other end I was losing my grip on the present. All I knew was that Rick looked beautiful, stark naked and poised just in front of me. He seemed so casual about it, too, thighs flexing while he bent down to tidy up his discarded clothing, stuffing his socks into his boots, and folding his jeans and t-shirt before setting them down on the chair. He reached out and took the plug from me again.

"This what you wanted?" he asked, holding the plug beside his cock so I could see. He was thicker, but not by much. But the plug itself by comparison seemed like nothing more than a silly toy with it's shiny surface. Too perfect and pretty compared to the raw, throbbing length of flesh that Rick still gently held by the tip to give me a full view of it. He even turned slightly so I could catch another angle. He was thicker from the front than from the side.

I blinked, trying to articulate a response between my fascinated observation of him. But all I could think about was that if, somehow, I could accommodate the width of that plug, then I could probably, *almost* take Rick's cock, too.

"What do you think? Too much for you or do you want to try again?"

I could only nod. Rick smiled and passed the plug off to Max again. A fresh, cold squirt of lube hit my ass followed by the pressure of the heavy, tapered tip of the plug. I relaxed and closed my eyes. My breathing accelerated with each slow push of it into me. It was more than uncomfortable, in spite of the lubrication, and I loved it. My clit throbbed harder the more my ass was stretched. Just when I feared it would tear me in two, the vibrator kicked on and my core exploded into sensation. All at once, the plug slid deep, the harsh stretch subsided only slightly but was replaced by a solid fullness, and Max's fingertip found my clit and rubbed it just as perfectly as he had the night before after spanking me. Only this time he used his other hand to rain down a steady, quick series of blows against each ass cheek in quick succession.

I screamed my ecstasy and reached my arms out blindly. Rick grabbed my hands and squatted down before me. Through the haze of pleasure all I saw were his blue eyes and gold hair. I wasn't sure if I said anything—all I could think was how much I wanted his mouth on mine, and then suddenly it was there, his lips pressed hard and his tongue meeting mine as I hungrily devoured his kiss, using him as the anchor to carry me through the most intense orgasm I'd ever had in my life.

CHAPTER ELEVEN

*R*ick stayed with me, the kiss growing slower and more tender as my body's spasms gradually subsided. I was only vaguely aware of my surroundings, but acutely attuned to the sensations around my hips. Max's hand rested lightly on my sore backside.

His voice was rough when he said, "You all good, baby?"

"I think so," I said. I gasped in response to the tugging, slipping sensations of both vibrator and plug being removed from me, the slick friction lighting up my already sensitized flesh. Their absence left me feeling empty. Then Rick was gone, too, and for a moment everything was too solitary and quiet for me to process. I cried out an objection but it faded from my lips when a pair of hands tugged at my shoulders, urging me to stand.

I did, and found myself wrapped in Max's strong arms. I nearly collapsed from dizziness and confusion when I found my feet, but he caught me and sat, tucking me onto his lap. I let myself sink into him, pressing my face against his chest, my entire world focused on the close-up of the dark inkwork that framed his collarbone. His hands slid over my skin in gentle caresses, avoiding sensitive areas. After a time my breathing felt less irregular and the room finally came back into focus. I realized that my weeping pussy was probably destroying his leather pants, not to mention the sticky residue of the lube that remained on the backs of my thighs. All those sensations seemed beyond my comprehension, though, and I wasn't quite sure how to deal with them. Max didn't seem to mind, though, so I decided I wouldn't worry about it, either.

I let out a slow, stuttering breath and tilted my head up to smile at him.

Max smiled back down at me, his face filled with concern that barely concealed a raw need. His cock was the next thing that drew my attention, its hard length pressed bruisingly into my hip, but he didn't seem to be as aware of its presence as I was.

"Are you thirsty?" he asked, reaching for a fresh water bottle. I nodded and he tilted the bottle to my lips for me to drink. His brows drew together and he looked thoughtful while I swallowed the water in thirsty gulps.

"I'd tell you if I wasn't okay with this, you know that, right?" I asked softly when he pulled the bottle away from my lips. "I want this," I said. "I love this."

His face relaxed and he rubbed my thigh. "We can take a break if you want, or try something different. It's up to you."

I eyed the bundles of pale rope Rick had left on the counter. "What do you do with those?" I asked, my mind already running through all the possibilities. There was a lot of rope so I had trouble coming up with scenarios that would require so much of it.

Rick wandered over and picked up one of the bound coils and released one end of it, letting it fall to the floor unwinding as it went. He'd put his jeans back on but they did little to conceal his arousal. I was every bit as fascinated by their reactions to me as to the potential fun we could have together next.

"We tie you up," Rick said. "My personal favorite part. I'm out of practice, though. If I'd known I would be doing this today I would have brought my camera."

"What? Why?" I asked.

Max shifted under me. "He used to have a reputation in our old circle for being the master of knot-work. Most popular bondage Dom at the club. And with work that elaborate, he'd make a point of recording it."

"I improvised sometimes," Rick clarified. "And I liked keeping a record. Never shared any of the videos, though. But if Chloe liked something specific, she usually wanted me to repeat it so I had to know what I'd done."

"What was your specialty at the club?" I asked, looking at Max.

He smirked at me and gave my thigh a light smack. "What do you think?"

"Oh," I said and smiled. "I like that. But I want to know what it's like to have both."

"You were cuffed to the bed last night," Max said. "Did you like that?"

I nodded. "But I have a feeling this is different, isn't it?"

Rick wandered toward us, trailing the rope behind him. He squatted down in front of me, and took both my hands, looping a doubled length of rope around my wrists and tugging until it was snug. The silken tails of the rope slid along my thighs, tickling as he wrapped the rope in uniform loops around my legs, binding them together at the knees. "This is very different. The process of tying you is half the fun. What we do when you're bound is the other half."

"We have a camera," I blurted. "Don't you want to record what you do here?" The idea of being tied up and at their mercy thrilled me, and the suggestion of also being able to see it all again later was every bit as enticing as the ropes themselves.

"Are you sure?" Rick asked.

I nodded. "It's my first time. I want to learn how to

do it, too. And I might not be paying very close attention while it's happening."

"You definitely won't see all of it," Rick said as he tied off the end of the bindings above my knees. "All right, where is it?"

"Hall closet upstairs," Max said, jabbing his thumb at the ceiling.

I looked down at my bound wrists and knees after Rick . "Um … I don't see how this is going to work." I plucked at the ropes wrapped snuggly around my thighs.

"Use your imagination," Max said. He urged me off his lap. I stood, a little unsteadily and uncertain where to go since I couldn't exactly walk. Max moved around me, adjusting the position of the chair so it was in front of me again.

"Bend over and rest your hands on the seat." He rested one hand on my shoulder and the other against my low back for balance, then slid it down over my ass as I bent.

"Like this?" I asked, locking my elbows and looking over my shoulder.

Max didn't meet my gaze, though. He seemed too absorbed in the view of my ass. I bit my lip, thinking I was starting to understand one of his tells. His palm still rested on one ass cheek and he idly rubbed in a circle. My pulse sped up and I arched my back, tilting my hips a little closer to him.

"You like being exposed like this, do you?" he asked.

"Mhm," I said, thinking he'd been far too gentle with me so far, in spite of the whipping I'd gotten, but all he would do was stroke my backside.

"I made a mess of you with all the lube. Let's get you cleaned up, why don't we. Don't move, baby."

"But …" I craned my neck but stayed put as I watched him stride off to the laundry room. I heard water running for a moment before he returned, a clean, wet rag in hand. The damp heat was a comfort on my sore flesh, but more than that I loved the tender contact as he cleaned the sticky residue from my skin. After several sweeps of the cloth, I no longer cared why he was touching me, only that he didn't stop. I lowered my head and closed my eyes, losing myself in the slow, gentle strokes of the cloth, up my inner thighs, around to my ass and over, without delving anywhere more sensitive for several passes.

I gasped as he made another pass and the rougher texture of a knuckle grazed my exposed flesh. My pussy ached again, and throbbed with heat wetter than the now cooling cloth. He pressed the soft terrycloth between my legs a little harder, holding it over my swollen clit before dragging it along my slit and up the crack of my ass. I wanted desperately to spread my legs, to let my pussy open for him to have better access. The inability to do so both frustrated and intrigued me. I didn't feel like I could get the contact I really wanted, but I loved what Max was giving me.

"Feels better to be clean, doesn't it?" His breath gusted hotly against my thigh and I quivered, briefly considered begging him to do whatever it was he seemed to be thinking of doing with his face so close to me.

Soft contact brushed my hot folds—too soft to be fingers—and something even hotter and wetter teased me deeper. I moaned at the delicious sensation of what had to be his tongue, exploring slowly up and down my cleft, all the way from my hood piercing up to my asshole and back.

In the periphery I heard Rick return, but he said nothing. I kept my eyes closed, simply wanting to experience whatever they decided to do to me without thinking about it.

"Are your eyes closed, Casey?" Max asked, his lips brushing against my sensitive flesh with each word.

"Yes."

"Good. Keep them that way."

His warmth and touch disappeared from behind me for a second and I could hear low murmuring, but couldn't make out their words. My fingernails dug into the cushioned seat of the chair I leaned on. Maybe I'd get the plug in my ass again, or … oh, God, maybe one of them would fuck me now. How would it feel with my legs bound together this way?

It was Rick's voice that spoke next, from somewhere in front of me. "Casey, I want you to know the camera's recording now. If it makes you uncomfortable, use your safe word."

I nodded.

"Respond out loud, please," Max said behind me.

"I- I understand. I asked to be recorded, didn't I?" I couldn't help the flippant tone in my voice, but the presence of the camera just added another layer of taboo to the entire scenario. Not only were my stepdad and his hot best friend in the process of doing very naughty things to me, but the camera made it feel like untold others might see it.

Rick chuckled. "That you did." His voice had moved closer and my eyelids fluttered open just in time to see him holding a swath of fabric in front of me.

"I'll keep my eyes shut, I promise," I said.

"Oh no. Promises aren't enough. We're going to make sure you keep your eyes shut for this. If you want to see it, you'll see it after it's over. This is the beauty of a recording."

He wrapped my eyes gently with the sheer scarf and tied it behind my head. I could still see through it somewhat, but could only make out shadows. Ricks shadow loomed closer just as Max gripped both my ass cheeks roughly, fingertips digging in and spreading me wide for his tongue to slide up and down my pussy with swift, lewd strokes.

Rick's musky scent filled my nostrils as he leaned close, his thick biceps brushing against my bare arms. With both hands, he cupped my breasts and my nipples went instantly hard under the teasing of his thumbs. He toyed with me for several seconds, his mouth against my ear whispering.

"Max said you would like this."

I almost replied with a sarcastic laugh and a playful retort about how horrible it was having my nipples teased. His hands slipped away and sharp twists of pain shot through my chest when the weights he'd attached to my hoops gave into gravity. I was forced to lean forward, but had trouble dropping low enough to relieve the pull—I could only go far as bent elbows.

I cried out in dismay, confused about what they expected but not yet ready to give in.

The sharp sting of the whip on my ass distracted me momentarily, confusing me even further.

"Down, baby. You know what you need to do to make it stop."

The switch whooshed through the air again, coming down in another sharp, stinging crack. I pushed my arms out in front of me, ignoring the burn in my hamstrings as I bent almost double to let my abused nipples rest on the seat of the chair. The stretch of my muscles was a small discomfort compared to the pain in my breasts.

The relief was instant, but also short lived as Max brought the switch down on my ass again. Only this time he followed it with a swipe of the smooth column of the switch between my soaked pussy lips, making sure to snag and tease at the piercing at the top of my clit.

The pleasure intensified when he took the switch away and replaced it with something hard and cool that spread my slit wide. Behind the blindfold I had no frame of reference for what he was invading me with, but whatever it was felt amazing. It was wider and smoother than his finger, but had the same amount of give to it. He rubbed it up and down, teasing at my sensitive nub until I gasped, my thighs shaking at the strain of the position.

I twined my fingers together, wishing for some-thing—anything—to hold onto. Being trapped in this haze of shadows had me feeling like a disembodied bundle of sensation and I needed something to ground me. A large hand slipped between mine and I gripped it, grateful for Rick's intervention. His warmth came down close to me again, mouth at my ear whispering once more.

"We're going to make you come. Then we're going to fuck that sweet little pussy of yours."

I gasped when, on the word *fuck,* the object Max had pressed against my clit slid deep into me, stretching my slick walls painfully wider than even his cock had the night before. The vibrator hadn't been big enough to leave a lasting impression, but whatever it was he was using on me now definitely wouldn't be forgotten.

My fingernails dug into Rick's hands and he tugged at my arms, forcing me to slide across the chair until my elbows plunged off the other side. I grabbed for him and he shifted closer, shoring me up with one strong shoulder against my chest and his breath hot on my neck while Max fucked me with something almost too big for me to comprehend. The first stroke stung on the way back out, in spite of how wet I knew I was. On the next plunge inside it transformed into more than pain. I clenched my muscles tight around it, testing the soreness of my muscles and finding I enjoyed the sensation the same as I enjoyed stretching the day after a hard work-out. I held tight to it when he slowly pulled it back out, enjoying the way its odd ridges rubbed at my insides.

"Jesus, baby, you must love this the way you're hanging on."

I could only whimper and pant into Rick's shoulder. Words failed me, particularly the dirty ones that came to mind. Even though they'd both seen me naked and falling apart at the seams already, finding the guts to scream, *"Oh God, fuck me now please,"* seemed like it would be a little too much.

I did manage to let out a guttural "Oh God" that was accompanied by a line of saliva against Rick's bare shoulder.

"That's right. Let go." His deep voice seemed

disembodied in my ear even though he was right there against me. With swift, sure strokes, he rubbed my back and swept his hands around to my breasts. The tug of the weights pulling on my nipples pinched when he released them from my hoops and then gently rubbed my hard, sore flesh with his fingertips.

CHAPTER TWELVE

I couldn't tell quite what it was that made me come completely undone. The hard thrust of the dildo was only half of it, but when it suddenly came to life with violent vibrations inside me at the same time as Max pressed a slick finger against my ass and shoved in two knuckles deep, I lost it. Every cell in my body became a white-hot glowing ember, exploding with sensation. I thrashed my head on Rick's shoulder and sunk my teeth into his flesh in a vain effort to stay sane. My knees locked and I had the vague sensation of warm wetness trickling down my thighs. I had the presence of mind for a split second to worry that I'd drawn blood and tried to pull away and apologize, but he'd twined his strong fingers through my hair at the back of my neck and slammed his mouth onto mine, holding onto me as though he knew exactly what I needed—a lifeline to keep me from transforming entirely into a cloud of disembodied particles and disappearing into the wind.

Rick broke away and with a soft tug, the blindfold came off my eyes. He looked almost as dazed as I felt when he peered into my face.

"You doin' all right, honey?" he asked, his mouth quirking into a shaky smile.

"I have no idea," I breathed.

Behind me Max slowly removed the dildo and stepped away. Water ran again nearby, and again a warm rag swept gently between my thighs, removing the slick evidence of my orgasm. He'd never be able to wipe away the experience, though, and I never wanted him to.

Rick removed my blindfold, undid the bindings around my wrists, then slid his hands up and gripped me under the arms to help me rise while Max swiftly tugged the ropes free from around my thighs. When I was sitting on the chair with them both squatting down in front of me looking concerned, I couldn't help but laugh.

Max gave me a perplexed look. "What's funny?"

"Both of you. Jeez, you're both so ... big and strong but you look like you're, I don't know, prostrating yourselves in front of me. What the heck did I do to earn this? I mean, I'm not complaining ..." I let out a shaky breath. "I'm still just *me*." I shrugged my shoulders and gave Max a hesitant smile, hoping he'd confirm one way or the other what I was only just beginning to understand about myself—that I really wasn't the Casey I'd been the day before, the girl hoping to find some way to understand what I worried were weirdly deviant desires.

Rick glanced at Max, who answered. "You're so much more than the girl you were yesterday, baby. So much more."

They watched me quietly as I chewed on my lip, struggling to clamp down on the uncertainty that threatened to ruin the buzz of euphoria infusing me at the moment. I caught sight of Rick's truck out the kitchen window and the real reason for his presence at our house barreled back. The sheaf of papers on the counter sat there, threatening me with their finality.

I had to think of some way for this *not* to end, but I knew the second my mom came back the following day, that would be the end. Max would be gone and Rick along with him, and every hope I had of under-standing myself, too.

"What is it, baby?" Max asked, leaning forward and laying a hand on my thigh.

"I just don't want this to end. Not today—or ever."

"We've got all day. We can do whatever you want, just say the word."

I nodded. I'd take advantage of the offer now, at least until I could come up with a better idea.

"You guys are the experts, and Rick said …" I bit my lip and glanced shyly at Rick. He raised an eyebrow, even though the amused look on his face betrayed that he knew precisely what I was thinking. He'd been the one to *say* it to begin with, after all. I took a deep breath. If I could be naked and enjoy getting fucked with a giant dildo, I could say a few words out loud. "Rick said you'd both fuck me. That's what I want, but … your way. I mean, tied up, but not blindfolded this time. I want to see you both."

"Lady's choice always is the most rewarding, buddy," Rick said, giving Max a smug look. He stood and grabbed a fresh coil of rope. "You recovered enough, or do you need a break?"

I shook my head vigorously. "Now. I want it all now."

Max nodded and stood, reaching out a hand to help me up, too. "You need to learn to pace yourself, but as long as you're not sore we can get started. We'll take it slowly this time."

The pair of them choreographed the next several minutes, positioning me by the table at first while Rick slowly and methodically wrapped ropes around my torso and tied intricate knots. Soon I began to feel like I was being bound up by some devious, kinky spider. Lengths of rope extended out in several directions from my body. Then they urged me to lie back on the table. The heavy glass and iron piece of furniture was pleasantly cool against my bare backside, the contrast a sweet reminder of the stinging strikes Max had given me throughout the morning.

A tug of the ropes pulled my hands back and my

body with them. Rick's gentle touch positioned my hands just so. I felt a little bit like a rag doll, being posed, but every slip of the ropes around my flesh sent more tingles of pleasure through my body.

"Lie back," Rick said, pushing me back toward the table and helping me to recline on the surface of it. A throw pillow caught my head and I let myself relax as he tested each stretch of rope over my skin, sliding his fingers beneath. I sensed that it was only a precautionary measure for him to check the tautness of my bindings, but every sweep of his fingers between my flesh and the ropes made me want more contact.

"Time for your legs," he said.

It became hypnotic, the slow testing of my position and the tickle of the rope sweeping around and around as he coiled and knotted repeatedly, the delicate insect caught in a spider's inescapable web.

He tugged one leg up and bent my knee. I let him, watching with abstract interest as he positioned my bent knees just so and wrapped the cord and knotted it with swift, sure motions of his hands—too fast for me to even track. He had the intensity of an artist, or at least of someone who knew precisely how to do what they knew best.

A stray length of the rope drifted between my thighs and I gasped at the contact. My pussy throbbed with the need to be filled again, but I'd managed to block it out while I focused on Rick's artistry. The wayward length of silk inadvertently stroking me reminded me with excruciating ecstasy how much pleasure I had already experienced that day, and promised of more to come.

"Oh, God," I said.

"Almost done." Rick sped up his movements and I gasped when he tugged a little too tight, pulling my left thigh against my torso. He loosened it again and eyed me. I nodded when the binding slackened enough and he tied a quick knot.

He let out a satisfied sigh and stood back.

CHAPTER THIRTEEN

"*I* think you've outdone yourself," Max said.

"I couldn't exactly skimp, all things considered," Rick said.

"I suppose not."

"Everything good, Case?" Max asked, moving closer.

"Yeah, I think? It's nice, but ... different." I wished I could've given him a more articulate response, but I was still absorbing the newness of the intensely arousing sensations Rick had left me with. My body was criss-crossed with knots and ropes. He'd managed to somehow bind my arms down to the table, stretched out perpendicular to my body, and my legs were tied up bent and spread wide, the position a sharp contrast to the closed-thigh position they'd had me in earlier. I couldn't see how they were tethered to the table, but it didn't matter. I could imagine how I looked, sprawled across the circular surface with my pussy bare and weeping.

All I knew was that I was fully exposed to the two of them and completely at their mercy. And my pussy felt like a molten pit just waiting for one of them to cool me off.

"You comfy, Case?" Rick asked.

"Pretty much," I said. "You've done this before, haven't you?"

Rick laughed and bent over me, resting his elbows casually on the table just above my bound arms. "Yeah, your stepdad and I were the go-to guys for awhile. But life happened."

"And you stopped for love?"

"You could say that. Now it looks like things may be coming full circle." His gaze flicked down over me, admiring his own handiwork. "Christ, Casey, you really are something else."

He stretched his hand out and toyed with the steel hoop that pierced one of my nipples. His touch was delicate at first, and deliciously arousing as he swirled his fingertips around and around in teasing circles. I watched his face slowly transform from businesslike to pure lust as he continued teasing, moving his fingertips in a line tracing the lines the ropes made in my flesh.

"Close your eyes, baby," Max said.

I glanced down my torso to where he stood. He rested both hands on my ankles and squeezed gently, sliding his palms up to my knees. I let my lids drift closed and gasped when he moved his hands and drifted them along my stomach downward until his thumbs grazed my slick lips. My senses came alive under their contact, with Rick's touch becoming more urgent, stroking my breasts and tugging at my nipples. After a moment his hot breath hit my neck and his soft lips trailed up along my jaw, finally coming to rest against my mouth.

The sensation of his tongue sinking into my mouth somehow grounded me and I lifted my head to meet him, sucking hungrily at his lips. He tasted like coffee and something a little sweet—honey maybe. I decided I liked kissing him as much as Max.

In the next moment I was grateful for his mouth on mine. Between my legs, Max's touch became more intense, his fingers stroking harder. I heard a slight rustle as he moved and then his hot mouth was on me, his tongue gloriously licking and sucking at my clit.

I moaned into Rick's mouth and sucked harder at his tongue. I wanted to move, to clutch at his hair, touch him, but bound down as I was, all I could do was flex my fingers and grip the edge of the table while Max sank his tongue into me and back out, teasing my pierced hood with tight, maddening circles.

My breath came in pants against Rick's mouth and he pulled away. I opened my eyes for a second, and met his intense gaze peering down at me.

"Let go, Case," he said and dipped his head lower to my breast.

Max's hands gripped my thighs while his mouth devoured my pussy. I cried out, my chest heaving, when his sucking lips pulled the climax from me in a long, tortuous flow of ecstasy that seemed to sink through my body from my outer edges to my very center.

Tears streamed down the sides of my face, soaking my hair as he continued sucking and drawing out my orgasm. In the split second after it subsided I heard the sound of rustling clothing and looked down again to see his erect cock free of his pants and aimed at my core.

"Yes," I murmured and smiled up at him.

He smiled back briefly, his expression becoming filled with nothing but pleasure as his cock sank into me.

Rick kept steadily stroking me, occasionally teasing his fingers just under the tight bite of the ropes where they cut into my softer flesh. Sometimes he would use his tongue on me instead of his fingers, leaving cool stripes of moisture behind each tickling taste.

Max began with slow, even strokes at first, barely moving as my still sore pussy acclimated to him for the second time. I winced at the reminder of the pain from the night before and he paused.

"Still hurt?" he asked.

I nodded. "Don't stop, please. I love that it hurts."

Rick's brow creased above me and he looked at Max then back down at me. "Were you … Jesus, were you a virgin?"

I gasped and closed my eyes when Max pulled out and shoved back into me with a deliberate thrust. My muscles spasmed around him, reawakened by the pressure of his thick length invading my inexperienced depths.

"Y-yes. Oh, God, like that. Do that again!"

Max chuckled and I opened my eyes again. I smiled up at Rick whose expression had taken on an awed, wondering look. "Lucky bastard," he said.

My eyes stayed fixed on Max, roving over his flexing muscles, now glistening with sweat. Morning sunlight shone off the gleaming steel hoops through his nipples. God, I wanted to do things to him with my mouth. I licked my lips at the thought.

"I think she needs something to occupy her tongue, don't you, baby?" Max asked.

I nodded, thrilled that he'd seemed to read my mind so easily.

"That can be arranged," Rick said. He leaned down and kissed me again, letting his lips slide across mine and teasing his tongue out to wet my mouth thoroughly. While his mouth was pressed to mine I heard the unmistakable sound of his zipper descending. He stood up a second later and I turned my head to watch him slip out of his jeans.

I couldn't take my eyes off him and he seemed to be able to tell how mesmerized I was. God, I'd just seen him a little while ago, but still wanted to just look. He reached one hand out and stroked my cheek gently, while sliding his other palm up along the length of that glorious pink shaft.

"You want a taste, Casey?"

"Yes."

The edge of the table was the only obstacle, but his hips were high enough above the surface that he could lean over slightly and aim the tip of his cock at my lips. He kept his hand resting gently on my jaw, his thumb on my chin while he guided his cock to my mouth. Max's steady fucking slowed and then picked up again along with a gentle rubbing at my clit.

Every single one of my senses came alive with the first flick of my tongue along the glistening slit at the tip of Rick's cock. He was a little bitter like coffee the first time I'd tasted it, but mostly salty-sweet and I lifted my head to wrap my lips further around his tip. The skin was hot and so smooth. I wanted to taste more of him. I slid my tongue around the head, teasing at the underside like Max had shown me the night before, and then sucking gently, wishing for him to feed me more of his hot shaft.

He did, leaning over and bracing one hand on the table behind my head while he slowly lowered his hips toward my face, his cock sliding between my lips bit by bit.

"You just hum if you want me to stop, all right?"

I made an "mhm" sound and tilted my head up to take him deeper. He clutched at the back of my head with his hand.

"Oh Christ, don't move, honey. Let me do the work."

I "mhmed" again and relaxed, letting him support my head while he slid out of me and then back into my mouth until I could feel his tip nudging at the back of my throat.

"That's right. Fuck that pretty mouth of hers," Max said, speeding up between my thighs.

I moaned around Rick's cock, overwhelmed by the sensation of Max's thickness stretching my walls again and the smack of his heavy balls against my sensitive asshole.

His fingers worked my clit more deliberately, fresh zings of pleasure shooting through my body. They became more intense when a pair of hands clutched my breasts. Two different hands, this time. One pair of fingers squeezed harshly, causing delicious spikes of pain to shoot through my nipples. The other was gently teasing, the contrasting sensations sending me into a confusing whirl of pleasure until I wasn't sure which way was up.

"Holy fuck," Rick said and his thrusting into my mouth became jerky, suddenly sinking in a little too deep until I gagged and clenched my eyes shut tightly.

He abruptly pulled out of my mouth and let out a harsh groan.

I opened my eyes briefly, and he quickly covered them with his hand, but not before I caught a glimpse of his face contorted in pleasure and his other hand rapidly stroking his cock as creamy fluid spurted from the tip, landing hotly on my cheeks and lips.

Max's movements changed, his thrusting growing more violent. The harsh push of his cock into me, filling me so perfectly and the rub of his piercing along my oversensitized inner nerves made me wish I could wrap my thighs around him and hold him deep. He let out a loud cry and the sensation of his cock pulsing inside was the most erotic thing I'd experienced. He slammed hard into me once more and didn't move again except for the steady rubbing of my clit. One more tweak of my nipple and my body went soaring again, every nerve ending seemed to explode with my orgasm. I was abstractly grateful for the bindings holding me to the table because I was pretty sure if I hadn't been tied down, I'd have flown off into space from the pleasure of Max's wonderful cock filling me while Rick bent and kissed my cum-coated lips.

CHAPTER FOURTEEN

They didn't untie me at first. I didn't really care because I probably wouldn't have moved anyway. I watched in a daze as they donned their pants again and moved around the kitchen island. Water ran and a moment later the warm moist comfort of damp cloths began to rub gently at my sensitive flesh.

"Sorry about that," Rick said, wiping the soft cloth over my cheeks and lips. "At least I missed your eyes. That shit stings if you don't aim right." I smiled up at him and he grinned.

"I liked the way you tasted," I said.

He raised an eyebrow. "Oh? Well that's always a nice compliment. I bet you taste pretty sweet, too." He rested a gentle kiss against my lips and then began tugging at the knots in the ropes while Max cleaned between my thighs. My body quivered when he rubbed a little harder over the sensitive bundle of my clit. I moaned and tilted my hips up toward him.

"Hold off," he said, placing a hand on Rick's shoulder. "You want to taste her? I think she's good for another, aren't you Case? You want Rick's mouth sucking you off?"

My eyes fluttered shut at the idea of watching that blond head and those blue eyes between my legs, pleasuring me. I was too far gone to speak, simply tilting my hips up into Max's touch again.

Max chuckled. "I'll get the knots, you take care of her."

"My pleasure," Rick said before kneeling down again. He spread me wide open with his fingers and made a small humming sound before darting his tongue out for a taste. The hot, wet tip of his tongue teased just under the hood of my clit, toying with the piercing, then slid down and down, past my slick opening. He swirled his tongue lightly around my tight asshole, the unexpected sensation making me gasp in renewed pleasure.

He pulled away for a second, leaving his thumb against my tight, puckered opening. "Baby you're gonna love getting your pretty little ass fucked, I promise you."

Without another word he bent again and the slick tip of his tongue pressed harder, breaching that tight barrier while his fingers worked their way higher again. Two of them slid into my pussy while he pressed his thumb at my clit and rubbed in slow, hard circles.

The sensations were nothing at all like Max fucking me and the combination of them had me flying before I could even realize I was going to come again.

Rick looked dazed when he stood up and abruptly sat down on a bar stool. "Max, buddy, I hope you have a good idea how fucking special she is."

Max paused his methodical loosening of the knots that bound me. "I do now."

CHAPTER FIFTEEN

I spent the next half hour in the most amazing hot bath I'd ever taken. The pair of them urged me into it, in spite of my insistence that I was fine and wanted to help them load up Rick's truck with some of Max's things. But Rick stood guard at the door to my room while Max steered me into the master bathroom with its Jacuzzi tub, aromatic steam from Mom's expensive bath salts already filling the room.

I'd never really been what anyone would consider a spoiled child. Max was the kind of stepdad who refused to tolerate any bullshit, so I had learned quickly never to whine or complain about little stuff growing up. I'd learned what it meant to be tough from the best, and perhaps my enjoyment of being spanked was a reflection of that influence. I had no idea where my crazy desires originated. All I knew in those moments as he helped me strip out of the spare garment I'd been wearing all day and helped me into the bath was that I absolutely loved being pampered, and realized that I probably wouldn't have appreciated it so much if I'd been allowed to feel that way my whole life. Or if I hadn't been supremely sore, pretty much all over, from the exertion of the day.

"Trust me, you'll thank me for this later," he said into the steam, then kissed me on the mouth and shut the door behind him as he left. I stayed until the water cooled, then dressed and wandered downstairs to find them both sitting at the kitchen table, rimed with dirt and sweat and a pair of cold beers dripping condensation onto the tabletop … right onto the imprint my ass had left, I soon realized.

Max caught the direction of my amused gaze and smiled. "Yeah, we should clean that up before your mom gets home, huh?"

"Ya think?"

Rick stretched out an arm to me and I went, sinking onto his lap and enjoying the sharp scent of his sweat, mixed with the scent of wood, grease, and steel—the unique aura of a man who worked with power tools and lumber. They both smelled the same, I realized, though different in their own unique ways. I guessed it must be their taste in soap that differentiated them, at least in that one small way.

I rested my head against Rick's shoulder, my eyes catching sight of the dark bruise on his neck.

"Oh, shit!" I sat up and touched the mark. "I'm sorry about that," I said, grimacing.

"I'm not," he said. "Battle scars are my favorite. Don't tell me you don't have a mark or two from today. Would you have done things any different to avoid them?"

I thought about the pleasant tingling of my bottom as well as the slight raw spot on the inside of my wrist where I'd forced the ropes to rub me a little to much. "Not at all," I said. I turned to look at the camera, resting half out of its case on the counter.

"Can I keep the memory card?" I asked.

Max took a long swig of his beer, his Adam's apple bobbing in his throat as he swallowed. He always liked to stall an answer when I asked for something, but I could tell from the lines between his eyebrows that he'd heard me and was considering the question. I'd never been one to beg, though. The first time I tried it, I got my ass smacked by him and told that under no circumstance should I debase myself for *anything*. "It makes you look cheap, baby. You're too good for begging." I'd had to go look up the word "debase" just so I knew what he meant.

"It's yours," he said when he set down his bottle.

I frowned at the return of the sadness in his eyes, but this time he didn't have the desperate edge he'd had the night before when I'd found him in my room. Now he only looked wistful, and it made my heart ache to see.

"Daddy ..." I said, overcome with the need to comfort him and momentarily forgetting his insistence that I not call him that anymore. I moved off Rick's lap to move to Max. He let me come and exhaled harshly when I wrapped him in my arms. "I don't want you to go."

"No other option," he said. "It's been a long time coming. I suppose it figures that you and I would have found out ... how much we have in common now."

I sank against him with a nod and a sigh, enjoying his strong arm around me. Rick stood and opened more beers, handing me a fresh one, which I sipped slowly while the pair of them talked in subdued tones, focusing on the past they'd shared that I had never heard about before. They pointedly avoided talk of the present, or the future, even though during the conversation whenever the name "Aurora" came up, Rick would look at me with what I could only describe as appreciation. It occurred to me how rarely they might have been able to even talk about those days. Their old secret that neither of their wives had ever known about. But now I was a part of their inner circle. I simply drank and listened, happy to be learning more about Max and the things that made him who he was.

My exhaustion hadn't even registered until I found myself being carried up the stairs, half asleep. I protested when Max made to leave me alone in my bed, grabbing onto his hand before he left again.

"Stay, please," I said.

"You're exhausted, Casey. Learn to pace yourself. We'll have other days, I promise."

He turned off the light and left the door open a crack when he walked out. I wanted desperately to follow him, but my body failed to respond.

CHAPTER SIXTEEN

I could swear I only blinked, but the next time I opened my eyes, the light had changed. The hallway was dark, the house silent and the street outside still. It was still enough to hear the sounds from the master bedroom. Sounds that I'd heard before, but that made a cold weight settle in my belly.

I slid out of bed and padded across the hall. The sounds were louder as I approached, soft, feminine sighs followed by gruff, masculine moans. I thought I might throw up before I even reached the door to my parents' room. I hated myself for looking now, after all the times I'd heard them together and been fascinated by their noises, wondering what exactly they were doing. Now, I just felt sick because even though I'd heard them before together, I had never actually *cared* so much about it.

The door was slightly cracked and I peeked in. Immediately I wished I hadn't. There were candles lit —the scented ones that were only ever burning when Mom was home. I had just enough of a clear view of the bed to see her, naked and astride him with her back toward the door. Her ass was in plain view and his hands made dark shapes against her paler flesh while she undulated her hips over his.

Bile rose in my throat and it was a struggle to tear my gaze away quietly enough to escape.

I tore back to my room and dialed Sarah, desperate to escape this fucking house, but she didn't answer. It was 1AM, I realized, and her parents had a strict "no call" rule after midnight. I tossed my phone onto the bed and began throwing clothes into a duffel anyway. I didn't give a shit where I went. I just had to get *out*. Away from them. Away from my ridiculous fantasies somehow. I'd been a fucking fool all day. A stupid girl playing pretend with her fantasy hero. *Heroes*, I reminded myself through a haze of tears.

My other hero was still out there … Rick. I didn't have his number in my phone, but I damn sure knew where he lived, and I could walk there. If anyone would know how to deal with this, I hoped he would. Max and Mom could fucking burn in Hell for all I cared.

On my way through the living room the previously cloying walls seemed to fall away. After the last day I knew without a doubt that I didn't belong here and that realization in itself was liberating. I stopped and looked around, staring at all the mundane objects in turn, simply trying to find some meaning in them, but I couldn't. When my eyes rested on the wide-screen that hung on the wall, I halted, struck by a genius of an idea. Hell was probably a little different for everyone, but I was willing to bet my Mother's personal hell might be enhanced by some of the things I'd done recently. I pulled the tiny memory card out of my bag and slipped it into the reader in our media player, flipped on the television, and set the volume just high enough that it wouldn't disturb the neighbors, but that anyone in the house who wasn't sleeping could hear it. At least if they stopped having sex long enough to not drown out the sounds of my orgasms.

I almost stopped to watch, captivated by my own voice saying words I'd said only hours earlier, even though it felt like eons to me.

"*Respond out loud, please,*" *Max said.*

"*I- I understand. I asked to be recorded, didn't I?*" *I responded.*

"*That you did.*" *Rick sat holding the scarf before me, ready to tie it to my face.*

"*I'll keep my eyes shut, I promise,*" *I said.*

"*Oh no. Promises aren't enough. We're going to make*

sure you keep your eyes shut for this. If you want to see it, you'll see it after it's over. This is the beauty of a recording."

I LEFT the recording running as I walked out the door. My eyes were wide-fucking-open now.Book Three

PART III
SURRENDER

CHAPTER SEVENTEEN

"*C*asey, wake up, honey."

The warm hand on my shoulder jostled me out of a restless sleep. I blinked into the morning sun streaming through the window of Rick's pickup truck, then looked over at him where he stood peering through the driver's side door.

"Where am I?" I mumbled.

"You're in the cab of my truck. How you got here is something you'll have to answer, though. You sure weren't in it when I parked it last night. Is there something you want to tell me?"

I clenched my eyes shut trying to block out the memory of what I'd seen the night before. After the most amazing and eye-opening sexual experience of my life, I'd discovered the man who had orchestrated it having sex with my mother. True, he was still technically married to her—he was my stepfather, after all

117

—but he'd given me every indication that their relationship was over before he went to bed. Alone.

Even my sealed eyelids couldn't hold back the tears. My throat tightened up like a noose had just been strung around it and I could only shake my head.

"Hey, honey. Something must've set you off after I left yesterday. Come inside and talk to me, okay?" My stepdad's best friend was the sweet, honorable, heroic type. He squeezed my ankle and reached across the gearshift to grab the duffel bag I'd tossed in the floorboards when I'd climbed into the truck the night before. I'd meant to go to my friend Sarah's house, but she'd been unavailable, in spite of our near constant communication since turning eighteen and our subsequent high school graduation. We had big summer plans now that we were officially adults. Mine had mostly involved trying to understand some of the darker thoughts I had about sex. But I had a feeling all that would be changing now that Max and Rick had opened my eyes up to the true wonders of the BDSM world. At least that's what I'd gone to sleep imagining last night.

The humiliation of the experience was still acutely with me. Seeing my stepdad Max in bed with my mother again after we'd talked about how over their marriage was … his hands on her … it had all been too much. I couldn't stay in the same house with two people I couldn't bear to look at after the events of the last two days.

I let Rick help me out of the truck and lead me to his front door, my eyes hazy from tears. I had always adored his house, but had trouble appreciating the architecture of the Craftsman style bungalow my family had visited so many times for barbecues before Rick's wife had died a year ago. He'd built the house himself before even meeting his wife. My stepdad had helped him, and I still remembered coming around sometimes with Mom while the pair of them were in the middle of some project or other. Laying the plumbing or hanging drywall. It had been when I was too young to appreciate how gorgeous the two men were without shirts, but I could still recognize their masculinity even that young, and I loved being around them. I'd felt safe, protected.

It was a far cry from how I felt now. Max had betrayed me. And my mother … why was she acting that way if she was *divorcing* him?

Once inside, he urged me onto the sofa. I flopped down and buried my face in my hands, trying to hide behind the tears.

"Was it too much for you yesterday?" Rick asked softly. "The first session can take a lot out of you. I was a bit of a mess the first time Chloe dominated me. Felt like such a baby for a few days afterward. The second time was very different, though."

I shook my head. "It wasn't that. I loved it." Those were the only words I could get out before emotion bubbled up again at a fresh image of Mom's naked back hovering above Max on their bed. Rick left the sofa next to me and a moment later a box of tissues hovered in front of my face. I gratefully grabbed the box and he sat on the coffee table in front of me, resting his strong, calloused hands on my bare knees.

"Take a deep breath, honey. Talk to me."

"Mom … came home," I said, the words coming out in a stutter. I blew my nose and tried to catch my breath for more. "Last night … I saw them … together. Why would he do that?"

Rick's lips tightened, his jaw clenching tightly. "He wouldn't, Casey. I know Max."

"Oh yeah? Well I know what I saw!" I yelled at him, standing abruptly. "She was naked and … on top of him."

"When did you see this?" he asked, his voice harsh and serious.

I shook my head, trying to remember. I'd woken up in the middle of the night but couldn't remember what time it was. Late was all I knew. Then I remembered trying to call Sarah.

"About one a.m."

"Want to know something?" Rick asked. "I crashed hard last night when I got home. Not even a fucking hurricane could have woken me up, and your dad … er … Max did more work and was under more stress than I was yesterday. He's not a light sleeper, Case."

"He was touching her."

"Tell me *exactly* what you saw."

"He was lying there … and Mom was on top of him … and his hands were holding her."

"Like, on her tits? Were they kissing?"

"Why the hell are you asking me all this! I fucking saw them together, doesn't that mean anything to you?"

He sat back with a huff of exasperation. "Yes! It means a lot because he was so fucking devastated when he found out she was leaving him. Not only was he afraid that he would lose you in the process, she's also been fucking someone else. They haven't been happy together for a really long time. If your mom pulled something like this I doubt he'd respond the way you think he did. He loves you, Case, so I don't believe it happened the way you describe. Just try to remember. Humor me."

I shook my head, confused and trying to remember exactly what I had seen. The effort distracted me from the emotional aspect of the memory. The door had only been cracked a tiny bit, but just enough for me to see the candlelight flickering over my mom's naked backside. I really hadn't seen much more than that, though. The only parts of Max that had been in view were his hands holding onto her ass, which was *moving* on top of him. On top of the covers. My eyes widened at the memory, then my mouth dropped open and an icy stone sank into the pit of my stomach.

"Oh, God. I think I really fucked up."

CHAPTER EIGHTEEN

*R*ick's shoulders relaxed, but his look of concern didn't leave his face. "It's all right, just a misunderstanding."

"No! I mean I *really* fucked up. I left the memory card from the camera there ... I left it playing on the TV when I left the house."

Rick went white, then stood and left the room. He came back with his phone to his ear. "Maybe they didn't find it," he said, but he didn't sound very convincing and I gave him a dubious look. He shrugged at me. "It's still early."

After a second he looked at the screen of his phone and tapped swiftly. "He's not answering. Let's hope he gets the text."

He sat down again, even more tense than he'd been while interrogating me. He hunched over his knees staring at the phone.

"Shit."

"I'm sorry. I was just so … hurt. I wanted to hurt them back."

"I know, honey. It's just that Tanya never knew a thing about what we did *before*. We both made a promise to leave it behind after Aurora. That was such a goddamn clusterfuck, and not in the good way."

"But you guys are both so good at it. Why?"

He sighed. "After Aurora left, that whole world just didn't fit with the lives we envisioned for ourselves. We were really happy with the decision for a long time, too. I'm not sure what happened between Max and Tanya. I thought he'd found something like I had with Corinne, but the last few years have been so much different for them. You'd have to ask him about it, if you want the details."

I snorted. "If he ever talks to me again." A despair even worse than the hurt of betrayal filled me. I stared at Rick's phone where it rested on the coffee table now, willing it to buzz or ring or something to let us know Max had gotten the message. At the same time I dreaded hearing from him and having to endure his disappointment.

"Is it charged?" I asked.

"Yeah, it is," he said. He raked his fingers through his hair.

"What happens if I really screwed up?"

He looked at me, his face softening in response to my defeated tone. "Don't think about that yet. Let's wait and see what he says. We'll figure it out. Do you want to call someone to stay with in the meantime? Your friend Sarah maybe?" he asked.

"I tried calling her already. Do you mind if I stay with you? Her place is a nuthouse with all her little brothers and sisters. I'd kinda rather have some peace and quiet, if that's all right."

"Sure, stay as long as you want," he said. "Guest room might be a little dusty, but it's made up."

I gave him a grateful smile when he led me upstairs. He opened the door to the guest room and held it for me to enter. When I brushed past, my shoulder grazed his chest and he inhaled sharply. The awareness of him and the events of the previous day crashed back suddenly, drowning out my anxiety. I looked up at him, halfway through the door, my senses awash in his warmth and the musky scent of him.

I felt dizzy, lost for a moment in his intense blue-eyed gaze. He looked tired, the creases at the corners of his eyes deeper than I remembered them being, but he was still as gorgeous as always. More so, now that I had this new perspective on him and Max. Now that I'd been so intimate with them both. My chest felt tight, my breath caught halfway out of my lungs, my entire body tingling with the closeness of him.

"Case," he said, his voice rough. He seemed poised to retreat, his back pressed hard against the door jamb. His lips parted as though he were about to say something else, but all that came out was the pink tip of his tongue, sliding over his lower lip as his gaze drifted down to my mouth. His Adam's apple bobbed as he swallowed, then he shook his head as though to clear it. "No, honey. I'm fine with you staying here but until this thing with Max gets worked out there's no way in hell I'm touching you."

"Rick, I didn't …" I stared at him, not sure what to say. I was just *looking* at him—and really, really wishing he would kiss me. "I'm sorry," I said, my face heating with shame. My throat constricted and tears welled up. I stared down at my feet, but out of the corner of my eye I could see the bulge at the front of his jeans. My brows clenched in confusion. Did he want me or didn't he?

"Fuck, Casey, look at me." His rough, calloused fingers touched my chin. "You're an amazing young woman, but this is very new to you and one thing you have to understand is that there are *rules.* I don't mean just in the BDSM scene, either, but in life. You're Max's stepdaughter and you've been through one hell of a day. Even if you were clear of him, you're off limits to me until I know you're both okay. Besides, I know how much he loves you. This isn't over yet, I'm sure of it."

"So you do want me?" I asked.

"Not that it's relevant, but yeah. More than anything." With that, he turned his head and nodded toward the staircase. "Anyway, I can't be stressed on an empty stomach. You hungry?"

"Starving," I said. It was the truth—I'd eaten very little the day before, but mostly I was simply grateful for the distraction from—well, *everything*. Food was probably the best distraction. Rick gave me a comforting smile, patted me on the arm and headed back downstairs.

I spent a little while trying to decompress. I was curled on the bed staring out the window when my phone buzzed with a text from Sarah.

"Sorry, hun, crazy morning with the family. What's up?"

"Crazy morning with the family here, too ... call me?"

"So was Max pissed the other night?" she asked without preamble when I answered the phone.

"You could say that …" I said, then proceeded to give her a blow-by-blow of my evening after I'd seen her last, and the morning that followed. Sarah and I had been close enough for long enough that we had few secrets from each other. However, I grew a little worried when she didn't say anything for a moment after I stopped talking. "Are you there, Sarah?"

"Holy shit, Case. Holy *fucking* shit. I don't know whether to be jealous of you or happy for you or what. *Both* of them? At once?"

"Did you even hear the last thing I said? About Max and my mom?"

"Okay, that's pretty messed up, but put yourself in his shoes. He's hurting. I bet Rick's right—if your mom's been screwing around he wouldn't have done that. I mean he's *Max*. Sir Galahad couldn't be more *honorable.* And what you said about Rick? The guy sounds like he's as rocked by you as your stepdad but he won't touch you. Two peas in a pod those two. No surprise they've done that before. Holy shit is that *hot.*"

"You're not helping," I said. "What should I do now?"

"Wait it out. I'd offer to let you come here but you seriously don't want to be here. Josie's been having a tween tantrum for the last two days and Mom took away her Bieber as punishment. The boys keep taunting her with off-key serenades outside her room. I'm honestly surprised they even know the words. Not that 'baby baby' is hard to remember." She let out a snort of amusement. "No, stay there. Try to relax. I'll come by tomorrow and we can talk about the trip next week."

"Sounds good." I hung up feeling marginally better. The prospect of the summer trip we'd been planning lifted my mood even more. Being able to get out of town entirely would hopefully allow me to figure things out, regardless of what happened with Max and my mom.

a soft knock sounded at my door a little later.

"Come in," I said, my heart suddenly pounding at the very thought of seeing Rick again after the moment we'd had earlier.

He opened it up a crack and ducked his head through. "Food's ready."

I followed him downstairs, forcing myself to put my worries on the back burner at least until I ate something. Without hesitation he handed me a chilled beer and sat down with his own. It was such a normal thing for him to do, but I still stared at him for a second before sat down at the table. Within a few bites of delicious waffles with fruit and whipped cream, the sense of normalcy returned.

"Thanks," I said, giving him a smile.

"To a grown-up Casey," he said, clinking his bottle with mine, a twinkle in his eye.

I rolled my eyes at him. "I feel like a dumb little girl right now. Thanks for having patience with me today."

"My pleasure," he said. "And you're not dumb. Just complicated. What we do is not an easy thing to come to terms with—once you figure out what you like."

I let his words sink in while we chowed. After we finished eating, he opened fresh beers and we relocated to the living room. I got the sense that he was trying to distract me from the fact that Max still hadn't called, but he was doing a poor job of it. Every few minutes he'd pull out his phone again and check the screen for some sign.

"He's not even answering you, is he?" I asked. "Do you think it's bad?"

He gave me a sidelong glance, hesitated, then seemed to come to some kind of conclusion. "It must be pretty serious for him not to call. Tell you what, if we don't hear from him after a couple more hours, we'll head over and find out what's up. Chances are he's just working things out with Tanya, though."

He flipped on his widescreen and tuned to a home improvement show. It was perfectly banal and mindless. After having my fill of food and beer, I sank back into the cushions, buzzed and sated.

"This guy's good," he said, turning up the volume to listen to the contractor talking about dovetail joints or something.

"He's cool," I said. "Not as hot as you, though. You should have your own show."

"I think you have to be gay to have a show on this channel."

"You and Dad … er … Max never, ah …" I paused, embarrassed at the question I was asking but unable to stop myself.

Rick barked out a laugh. "Well, I admit the man has his charms, but no, we've never been that intimate. We're both pretty low on the Kinsey scale."

"Oh, right," I said, frowning and pretending I knew what he meant. "I just figured since you guys get naked in the same room that you liked all of it."

He gave me an odd look. "Why do you look disappointed?"

"I'm not! It's just …" My neck and cheeks grew red hot as I struggled to find an excuse for my expression. "I think it would be really, really sexy is all."

Rick's eyebrows shot up practically to his hairline. "How much do you know about *that*?"

I scowled defensively. "I know what I like! And I'm figuring out I like a lot more than I thought, too."

He took a slow swig of his beer, his eyes narrowing while he regarded me thoughtfully. Finally, he said, "We're definitely open minded guys. You have to be to do the things we do, but we know what we like, too."

"Tying girls up, but not … touching each other?"

Rick tensed. "Tying *women* up," he corrected. "You may be a tad young, but you're an adult. Old enough to make the decision to do what you want, at least. Age isn't usually an issue, as long as a woman is over the age of consent. We've never had a sub as young as you, but we've had older women. What Max did with you the other night was probably poor judgment on his part, I won't deny it. And if I'd been there it wouldn't have happened that way. We don't go into a scenario with heightened emotions. The way he started with you was backwards, but I believe we did the right thing by not letting you try to figure it out on your own."

"I'm glad you stood up for me then. Thank you," I said, very conscious that he'd evaded the other half of my question with his little lecture. "But what if I want more than to be tied up and spanked? What if I want to watch you two do things?"

Rick shifted forward to prop his elbows on his knees and turned his head to look at me. "Everyone's desires and limits factor in, in one way or another. We always outline our limits when we start. Max and I have a few hard limits, and you should, too."

"So, touching each other is a hard limit?"

Rick's face turned bright red and he chugged the rest of his beer. "Not exactly," he said, his voice cracking comically. "Jesus, Casey, is that something you really want?" He stared at me, his eyes wide with a strange mix of excitement and anxiety.

"I'm not sure. I just know I like looking at you both naked, and I saw a video when I was at Sarah's house and her parents were out …" I shifted in my seat, embarrassed again to share more details of my curiosity with him, but to hell with it. After the last day why shouldn't I go for broke? I stared him down. "It was a video of two men, fucking a girl. And they were both, I mean their—ah—*hard-ons* were both inside her at the same time, and they touched each other in other ways, kissed."

Rick's lips parted, his tongue darting out. He tilted his bottle to his lips again before realizing it was empty. "Porn tends to be unrealistic," he said off-handedly, then eyed me with interest. "But you liked that? You think you want to try it?"

I nodded. My pulse hammered in my temples and between my thighs at the very idea of having them both fill me up that way. I already knew Rick had plans for my ass, and I wanted that, too, but this was something I'd fantasized about repeatedly since I'd seen it.

He cleared his throat. "So, now that I have a good idea of what you're interested in, I can try to make it happen. No promises." He gave me a stern look. "Now we need to make sure we know exactly what you *don't* want to do. Anything and everything that comes to mind is worth mentioning."

He proceeded to run down a list of some of his own hard limits, many of which made me grimace and shake my head vigorously, agreeing that those were *obviously* hard limits for me, too.

"People *like* to be *peed on*? And *strangled*?"

Rick nodded sagely. "We are nothing if not a fickle race of creatures. But you can feel free to try anything and rule it out as we go, *except* for those things Max and I won't do. If you really need something like that, then we'll have to talk about it first."

CHAPTER TWENTY

The conversation cheered me up drastically with the suggestion that there might be more to come, especially that he didn't consider my little fantasy a hard limit. But the lull we hit made me remember that we still hadn't heard from Max yet. Rick got up to get a fresh beer for himself after glancing at my own half-finished bottle resting almost forgotten on the coffee table. When he got back he relaxed into the sofa, his head tilted back.

His lids lowered and he seemed like he was recalling a favorite memory. "You should've seen yourself all spread open." He opened his eyes and their blazing blue stare hit me hard. All the moments of his attention the day before came rushing back while he kept talking. "You were so perfectly comfortable with the situation, too. Christ, Casey, that sheer enjoyment of the moment is ideal in a sub. I'd have hated to see you go down the wrong path and wind up unhappy. Ever since you've grown up, it's been tough not to notice you."

I could barely breathe at this little revelation. "Do you think Max thought about me that way, too?" I asked, hopeful.

"If he did, he never said so to me. That's not something we'd have shared, either way. How do you tell your best friend you have the hots for this eighteen-year-old stepdaughter? We're not a couple old pedophiles. We like women, not little girls, and you sure came into your own over the last year."

I turned and rested my back against the arm of the sofa, pulling my legs up and tucking them beneath me. I wished I could touch him again, and not in a sexual way. I'd had sex for the first time, been spanked, tied up, had two different cocks in my mouth and two different tongues in my pussy, all within the last forty-eight hours. I was overwhelmed by the realization of how much I'd loved it, but right now I just wanted a hug.

"Hey, hey, come here," he said, his expression growing concerned at my darkening mood. He tugged at my hand and I fell against him, trying to ignore the fresh tears that rolled down my cheeks.

"I don't feel like I'm grown up, Rick. I feel *stupid*. Like I've made a mistake, even though I loved every single second."

He wrapped an arm around me and squeezed

tightly while I buried my face in his shoulder, inhaling the spicy scent of his deodorant. He and Max used the same brand, I realized, but Rick's scent was somehow still distinct. Like fresh-cut wood and varnish. It was the way his house always smelled, probably wafting in from his workshop. It had always been a comforting scent to me, and worked wonders now to calm me. It helped that he just sat quietly holding me and rubbing my back.

"Everyone feels that way at the beginning. You're learning what makes you tick. What your body wants when it comes to pleasure, and it just happens to be a little different than what the average eighteen-year-old wants. Let me show you something …"

He shifted and gently sat me back up before standing and digging through a cabinet beneath the wall-mounted television. He pulled out a small, square jewel case and popped a mini-DVD into his player, then returned to the sofa and sat, pulling me back against him.

"What is it?" I asked, my curiosity overtaking my emotions as I snuggled against him, comforted by his closeness.

"It's an old video Max and I made before we met our wives. Before it starts, just know that the girl you're going to see was only a couple years older than you are now and it wasn't her first session, but this is how Max and I like to work. It shows a bit of how tailored a scene can be to the participants, too. She's the last sub we were with."

My pulse raced in anticipation of what I'd see. Was this the Aurora they'd talked about? The screen flickered as the picture appeared, grainy at first before it cleared and focused on a king-sized bed that looked like it was in a swank hotel room—if the beds in swank hotel rooms had red satin sheets and steel rings attached to tall, iron bedposts. The sound kicked on with a blaring beat of music and Rick hurriedly lowered the volume.

"Sorry about that. This is the raw footage of a rehearsal, no post production, but everything that happens is real."

The lighting shifted around the empty bed, making me think someone was adjusting it for maximum effect, as though it were a stage.

"Strobe on," a voice off-camera said. My skin prickled when I recognized Max's familiar inflection and deep tone. The scene darkened and flickered in the disconcerting rhythm of a strobe light, with a black light underneath, highlighting hidden imagery with every flash. It was mesmerizing.

Someone laughed off-screen. *"I think that's gonna knock their socks off."*

An accented female voice replied adamantly. *"Fuck that. I hate strobes. Get rid of it."*

"Chloe wants it for the show, Aurora." Max again. *"What if we blindfold you?"*

Rick let out a low laugh next to me. "Fucking Aurora. Some performers take themselves way too seriously."

"Fine. Blindfold me, but you two owe me a favor after hours if I do this."

"Anything for you, Aurora." A different male voice, just as familiar, answered her. I glanced at Rick, but he seemed too enthralled to notice me, his eyes fixed on the scene like we were watching his own wedding video. I almost felt like I was intruding, but the prospect of seeing the two of them in action from a distance was too enticing to abandon.

The strobe stopped and a figure stepped into the frame. I recognized Rick by his swagger and the dark tattoos on his upper arms. The scruffy cheeks, faint laugh lines and curly blond hair I knew and loved didn't exist on the version of him that I watched on the screen, however. Instead he was a smooth-faced young man with a buzzed head and deep tan, wearing a pair of leathers like a second skin. He was still well-muscled and toned, but not as bulky as the guy sitting next to me. I let out a low whistle of appreciation at the younger version of him.

Rick chuckled beside me and tilted his chin toward the screen. "Wait 'til you see my partner."

"How old were you?" I asked.

"It's coming on thirteen years ago, so … twenty-eight when we made this. About twenty-six when we started trying the lifestyle. Anytime we weren't deployed, we'd spend weekends with a Dominatrix in the city. That would be Chloe. She isn't in this, though."

"You said you were her sub. Did you get tied up, too?"

"The best way to learn how to be a Dom is to submit to one. She did everything to me before I was allowed to do it to anyone else."

"But you weren't the … subs … in this, um … ." I bit my lip wishing I knew how to speak his language. I wondered if he had a video of that, but didn't dare ask.

"Scene," he finished for me. "No, this was Chloe's first public test for the three of us. Max and I had worked together for about a year already. Jesus, Chloe was more trying than our drill sergeant during boot camp at times. Every recruit should go through her for training, if you ask me. We'd learn a lot more sensitivity that way."

I snickered at his comment, but quieted when his jaw clenched. "You're serious, aren't you?"

He let out a snort and shook his head. "After the shit I've seen during service, I know a lot of it could have been avoided if we'd had her brand of discipline ahead of the military. She's the one who taught us how to be men. All the military teaches us is how to be overgrown boys with guns."

He took a swig of his beer and glanced at me. His expression softened.

"I don't regret any of it, if that's what you're thinking," he said. "Want another?" He pointed at the empty bottle that rested in my fist. I'd forgotten finishing it.

"Sure," I said, and released the empty. I watched him leave, too fascinated by the fully grown man now to turn back to the video. The sounds drew my attention, though, and it wasn't sex that I heard.

It was laughter.

CHAPTER TWENTY-ONE

hree figures were tangled on the bed, one was obviously female and all of them were more or less clothed. She writhed and giggled in the arms of two ripped men who were *tickling* her. Mercilessly, too, from the looks of it. One was Rick, but the other—

I expelled a sharp breath when the other man's face turned toward the camera and I recognized Max. He had a delighted grin on his face that completely disarmed me.

"Oh, God," I said, before I could stop myself.

The beer bottle came around in front of me and I took it without looking back at Rick. I could feel him bracing his hands on the back of the sofa behind me.

"Let me know if this is too much for you and I'll stop it."

Always considerate to a fault, I thought. Max was that way, too, and had been all my life.

"No, I want to watch," I said. "She looks so happy." *And beautiful,* I thought, watching the slender brunette wiggle under their attention. She was in a black lace negligee with matching panties and her dark hair flowed in tendrils across the red pillow.

"That was her thing," Rick said. "Everyone has something I guess. Tickling was what got her going."

In the middle of the writhing limbs and the infectious laughter things changed. I couldn't take my eyes off the screen now. The men exchanged a glance and while Max continued the tickle torture, Rick stripped her bare, leaving a twisting shape of naked legs and torso and breasts. She undulated under their continued torture, obviously enjoying every touch.

Then the ropes came out and my entire body tingled in recognition of them. The slide of the silk cords over my skin was emblazoned on my memory. Max continued tickling Aurora while Rick went to work. It couldn't have been easy considering how much she wiggled, but her movements and laughter transformed before my eyes into soft moans of pleasure accompanied by more twists of her shapely body.

Instead of tickling, Max was now sliding his hands over her limbs, gently urging her into a facedown position for Rick to wrap her wrists and ankles with the ropes. Aurora's arms stretched wide when Rick tethered them to the steel rings in the headboard of the bed. Max gripped her ankles and yanked them down, spreading her legs wide and holding them for Rick to tie them, too. Then Max slid his hands back up her legs slowly, pausing to massage her ass and dipping his face between her legs as though to taste her. He left the frame after that, and all I could see was Rick and Aurora, with his deft hands tying knots and pausing every so often to caress her skin.

"Not my best work, but I always tended to save the fancy stuff for the real show. That was all I needed for her." Rick's breath puffed at the back of my head, making my scalp tingle.

I opened and closed my mouth. If what I saw wasn't "the fancy stuff" then what did my own tiedown mean? I'd been cocooned in ropes, but Aurora only had them around her wrists and ankles.

"Pay attention, you can learn something here. Particularly how different she is from you, and why you're a better fit for us," Rick said. His weight left the back of the sofa and I craned my neck around.

"Spoiler much?" I shot at him, then turned back to the screen, irritated, but secretly excited to know he thought I was a good fit—and for *them*.

Rick laughed and leaned back down behind me. One of his hands brushed my shoulder. I tensed and shifted away. We shouldn't touch, even as much as I wanted him to touch me just now, I knew better, and so did he.

His hand disappeared and he moved away. The image on the screen monopolized my attention.

Aurora was blindfolded and bound, and both men hovered over her with different implements of torture. Rick held a large plume-like feather, while Max wielded a leather thing that looked like it might feel soft until he reached back and let it slap against Aurora's ass with a smack. The broom-like tendrils of leather slid along her ass, caressing and making her twitch and moan. He lifted his hand and brought the whip down again, this time hard enough to leave red marks on her ass.

I hadn't seen Max's face the night before when he spanked me. Seeing it now, while he dealt steady, stinging blows to Aurora's ass, was like seeing him for the first time. He was younger, and more *there*. Every single movement he made was calculated to evoke a reaction from her. And every strike he landed did exactly what he hoped it would.

He always prefaced the strike with a steady tickle that made Aurora moan and twitch, while Rick steadily teased the feather all over her.

I wished I was her. The realization astounded me when it rushed into my head. God, I wished like hell I was her right now. I'd *been* her for a little while, the day before. Now with Max's silence I worried all my dreams were up in the air. My stomach knotted again and a chill raced over my skin.

"I can't watch the rest," I said, standing up and turning away from the TV to find the remote.

"Why not?"

"Because it's *him.* It's you. And I want so bad to be her, but I'm not and I don't know if I'll ever get to be. God, do you have any idea what the last two days have meant to me? I've been so damn confused for so long about these things I want. Now that I've actually gotten a taste, I don't want to stop. But I know Max probably won't ever touch me again and it fucking *kills* me. And now you won't touch me either out of loyalty to him. It makes me feel like I'm—I don't know— flawed somehow because you don't want me."

Rick stood behind the sofa still, a pace back, with the remote control in his hand. "Watch it," he said. "Just let it play out, so you can understand us better."

I watched, my gaze fixed on Max's fingers plunging lewdly into Aurora's wet, pink snatch. Her hips bucked back against him and he smacked her with the leather tendrils.

"Aurora, you know the rules of the show, no coming until I say so."

"Fuck you, Max. I'm gonna ..."

She cried out and her hips bucked with her orgasm. Max cursed and Rick laughed. He untied Aurora's bindings, continuing to laugh the entire time. Aurora joined in a moment later, but Max scowled furiously.

"That's it, Aurora. I'm done with you."

She giggled and wrapped her arms around him from behind, cooing in his ear. *"Aw, Max, lighten up. It was good for me."*

"No good for the club, though. We're entertainers, not your personal sex toys. If you can't take this seriously we can't work together."

"I don't understand," I said, staring at the screen.

"It was her prerogative to end the scene, but it was our livelihood at the time. She never quite fit our style as Doms, especially Max's, because she had real problems with authority. She needed a Dom who could work with someone like her. Max needed her full attention and respect to perform well. Chloe gave us an ultimatum—if we couldn't get Aurora to perform we had to find a new sub. We never did find another woman we could work with. I think you're that woman now. I hope so, anyway."

My stomach lurched. "You want me to … perform?"

Rick's eyes widened and he raised his hands. "No! It's not about that at all. Not unless you want that. You represent a lot for us, though … a way to make up for failing Aurora. She wasn't the right sub for us, but she needed more guidance than we gave her. And you're the first woman who's made complete sense with us."

The sound of a car door closing outside distracted Rick's attention. He paused the video and walked to the front door.

CHAPTER TWENTY-TWO

I tensed when I saw Max's familiar, broad-shouldered silhouette walking up the path outside the house. He looked worn out, beaten down, and entirely dejected, with a rucksack similar to the one I'd packed slung over one shoulder. Behind him in the driveway I could see his pickup parked beside Rick's and loaded up with even more of his belongings.

Rick opened the door for him and started to say something, but Max cut him off.

"Not in the mood to talk, man." He came in and tossed the bag on the floor before glancing at me but not saying a word. He didn't look angry, though—just tired.

"What happened?" I asked, unable to disguise my anxiety. I decided immediately after the words came out that I didn't really give a shit about my mother, or the night before. I was willing to trust Rick and give Max the benefit of the doubt, particularly now that I could see him.

Max collapsed into an overstuffed armchair and rested his head back, staring at the ceiling. "Well, your Mom got the point of your little gift, let's just say that. I spent half the day doing damage control when she threatened to call the cops and have both me and Rick arrested."

"What! But I said I was willing!"

"I know. She has nothing to go on, but she was damn upset about it. The rest of the argument was about the divorce and all the bullshit she could dole out with that as evidence. I finally convinced her to wait until she talked to you." He let out an amused chuckle followed by a sigh. "You should have seen her face. My God was that vindicating. I did feel bad for her, though."

"So … you weren't with her last night? I mean, I saw her in bed with you before I left. That's kind of why I did it."

He raised his head and looked at me, brows raised. "Jesus, Casey." He swiped both hands over his face. "I can't imagine how that made you feel. She ambushed me in my sleep. The whole night was pretty damn surreal, to be honest. After I put you to bed, I took something to help me sleep. When I woke up I was sure it was *you* straddling me and trying to ride me. The fact that I said your name when your mom was trying to fuck me was what set her off after that. I've been awake since about Midnight or so."

"Why did Tanya even come back last night?" Rick asked. "I thought you said she'd given you until tonight to move your things out. Not to mention she's with someone else now, isn't she?"

He shrugged. "She said she wanted a farewell fuck, for old times' sake. But the good sex Tanya and I had was history years ago. I don't envy the new guy, though. And I'm so fucking grateful Casey inherited her dad's personality."

"My dad? You didn't even know my dad, so how would you know?" I asked.

"I know enough about him from stories your mom told me before he died, and I found out more when I looked up his old squad mates. You're definitely not like your mom, you never have been. That's probably why I love you."

I was tempted to ask him exactly how different I was from her, but decided I really didn't want to know. Mom and I hadn't gotten along since I'd grown breasts. Max had ended up stuck between us through so many vitriolic arguments. Only half of them did he ever wind up coming out on my side of things, but he almost always had a good reason for taking her side, no matter how much I hated the fact.

Max's gaze drifted lazily over me and Rick, then moved to the paused image on the TV screen. He let out a soft snort. "A little lesson in what not to do, there," he said. "I can't believe you still have this recording."

"How long has it been since you watched this?" Rick asked.

"I burned my copy years ago."

"Yet you kept your gear. Why? Because you hoped we'd find another someday, but it never happened? Casey, tell him what you told me."

My eyes stung with tears again. I was relieved Max was talking to me but still anxious. I wasn't sure I could get all the words out a second time, but I took a deep breath anyway.

"I was afraid you wouldn't come back," I said, struggling to keep the desperation out of my voice. "I'm just afraid I'll never live up to the girl in that video, because I'm so new at this. When I thought you might be back with Mom, even after what she did—and what *we* did—it hurt. I don't want it to end, Daddy. Not when it just started."

His shoulders sagged when I finished. Just as I was about to escape upstairs to cry I found myself pulled into his lap and wrapped in his embrace.

"Jesus, Casey. I'm such a fucking fool. The last two days meant everything to me, too. I just couldn't reconcile it at first because—Christ—you've always been my little girl and now you're very much *not* that anymore."

"I want to be what she was to you," I said softly into his chest, pointing my chin toward the television.

He grabbed the remote control and killed the power with a curse.

"Screw Aurora. Forget you watched that, all right, baby? You're two very different women and *you* are the woman I want." His voice was gruff and intense in my ear, his stubble rough against my cheek. I took a deep breath and was calmed by his warm, familiar scent.

"Show me, please." I gazed up at him, hoping my face wasn't too puffy from crying. In spite of the dark mood, simply being held tight against his solid body had caused a low heat to grow deep inside me.

He slid his hands up my back, over my sweatshirt and cupped both sides of my face.

"I would do anything for you," he said softly, and my heart pounded when his lips pressed against mine. I savored the kiss, hoping it meant that he wouldn't abandon my cravings for the sake of propriety. He pulled away and gave me a small smile. "There's just one question I need to ask you," he said. "What do you want to try first?"

I blinked at him, then looked over at Rick, who leaned against the sideboard, hands braced on the edge. His lips were parted in anticipation of my words, his knuckles white from clenching the wood of the exquisite piece of furniture that I knew he'd built.

They both looked so beautiful, and they were hanging on my words.

"I just want to be with you both. Maybe make it up as we go—find our own rules. Is that okay?"

"That's the general idea, Case," Max said, giving me a wicked smirk. "Remember your safe word."

CHAPTER TWENTY-THREE

*R*ick led us up the stairs to his bedroom. Outside the door, he hesitated. "Ah, before we go in, you should know that I've been planning to get back into the scene, so I've been prepping a bit. It was the only thing that made sense for me after Corinne died. You guys will be the first to step foot in here since then."

The interior was a luxurious den that made my eyes widen in amazement. The king-sized bed was a work of detailed craftsmanship, with hand-carved posts that sported silver rings at varying heights. Midnight-blue paint covered walls that were draped with richly patterned silk and velvet. Along the walls were heavy wooden cabinets and racks displaying all manner of objects, few of which were familiar to me.

"Jesus, did you build that?" Max asked, pointing at the bed.

I was more interested in the trailing ropes that hung from several heavy steel rings in the ceiling. White silk lengths like the ones Rick had bound me with the day before hung down and trailed along the floor. I reached out a tentative finger and hooked one of the ropes, letting it slide through my hand.

"How do you use these if they're attached to the ceiling?" I asked.

"I can show you." Rick's warm hand rested at my waist, sending a thrill through me. "It's a little like what I did with the ropes yesterday, just with you suspended in air."

I could only nod, my mouth having gone too dry to speak the way my heart was pounding. My nipples pricked up beneath my shirt.

"That might be a little advanced for you, Case," Max said, coming up behind me with a concerned look on his face. Beneath his frown, however, was an eager look.

"You'll make sure we go slow, though, won't you?" I asked, giving him a smile.

"Let's get you naked then," Rick said, tugging at the hem of my sweatshirt.

My skin felt flushed when I stood there a moment later in all my glory between the two of them. Rick tugged at a dangling rope, pulling it free from the hoop.

"Kneel down here," he said, resting his hands on my shoulders and guiding me slowly to the soft rug that covered floor beneath the ropes. His touch was gentle but firm as he restrained my hands behind my back and began to slowly wrap my torso in the ropes so that my arms were held snug against my sides. The slide of the ropes over my skin set me ablaze again, like they had the day before.

He'd grilled me during our talk earlier on things I would or wouldn't be okay with, so I trusted him to be careful with me. Right now, all he was doing was tying me up, which was something I'd expressed was on my list of "hard limits of things I want".

"Spread your legs a bit more," Rick said. I did, and was rewarded by the soft tug as he passed several cords between my thighs and his fingers gently positioned them on either side of my bare pussy. He adjusted them until they were snug, leaving me feeling oddly spread open.

"Feel good?" he said in a rough voice, letting his fingertips slide along my exposed flesh between the ropes again, the contact making my core ache and the low burn of need deep in my belly grow even hotter. I closed my eyes and only barely managed to blurt out an affirmative that ended with a sharp gasp when he flicked lightly at my piercing.

Max sat on the end of the bed, watching intently while Rick worked. Soon my entire upper body from shoulders to crotch was almost covered in knotted ropes. Only my breasts were exposed, slightly squeezed at the top and bottom so they stuck out more prominently. Rick came around to the front with the end of a rope in his hand and paused long enough to drift his gentle touch across my breasts, flicking at my hoops idly.

Pleasure shot through my nipples, so much more acutely sensitive now due to the bite of the ropes into my skin. The touches came more frequently as he worked, some gentle and seemingly accidental, others more deliberate—a teasing stroke between my ass cheeks followed by the tickle of a rope over my shoulder or between my thighs. Every sensation layered upon the last one until I felt not only cocooned in silk ropes, but also in pleasurable touches.

"Are you comfortable?" Rick asked. He tilted my chin up and looked into my eyes earnestly.

"Yes, sir," I said.

He smiled. "I didn't ask you to call me 'sir' but I like it."

"I thought since you're a dom …" I started and stopped when he shook his head.

"I've never been a fan of that level of obeisance in a scene. If you enjoy it, by all means do it. My pleasure comes from simply restraining you and controlling your pleasure. I don't want to control your mind."

"Then yes, I feel really good, actually."

"Good," he said. "Now time for your legs. You're going to feel a little like a string puppet, but that's part of the fun. Just make sure to say so if anything hurts in a way you don't like."

He moved behind me again, and again the slide of the ropes worked its way over my skin. As he worked he attached ropes to my sides and strung them through the rings above me, gradually pulling them taut as he went.

"You're going to feel yourself lifted in a moment. Just relax and go with it. If I've done my job every- thing will feel comfortable."

"Okay," I said, having learned that a verbal response was preferred, where it was possible to give one.

My eyes met Max's and I smiled nervously. He returned the smile with only a nod as he stood and removed his shirt. He came toward me, his dark eyes intense. I had to crane my head up to look at him when he paused in front of me. He let his hand drift down over my head and cupped my cheek. I was acutely aware of the tight bulge that strained at the front of his trousers—the very idea of tasting him again made my mouth water.

"Can I have you in my mouth again?" I asked. The question provoked a small smile from him, but he shook his head.

"No, baby. I have other plans today. Are you in the mood for pain, too?"

If it was coming from him, I definitely wanted it. "Yes, sir," I said.

Rick moved behind me and my skin tingled when his hands slid down my arms again, gently checking the knots so far. A moment later I felt a tug at the center of my shoulders and at my hips, and the ropes around my torso tightened just slightly. I gasped at the odd feeling of weightlessness as I was lifted slowly off the floor, my legs unbending as I rose. A sense of vertigo hit as my shoulders dipped forward for a second then were pulled upright again with Rick's hand gently guiding my shoulder. The lifting continued until my feet dangled just above the floor. My ass felt suspended and stretched and I struggled, panicking at the lack of control I had over my own movements

A warm and rested on my back and Rick said, "You're fine, just relax. Does anything hurt? Anything too tight? Close your eyes and breathe, Casey. It's important for you to be aware *now* because you won't be in a few minutes."

In spite of the swaying vulnerability of my position I closed my eyes and tried to focus. Rick's hands were the first things I was aware of, holding my hips.

"I can feel you, where's Max?" I asked.

"Here, baby," he said. "I'm going to blindfold you, all right? You'll be more aware of your body if you're blind for a bit."

I opened my eyes just long enough to see his face before he wrapped a length of fabric around my head. Oddly, the blindfold let me relax a little. I couldn't see, so it let me focus on everything I could feel, and what I could feel felt amazing.

CHAPTER TWENTY-FOUR

I was surprisingly comfortable, suspended in the air as the pair of them held me from either side. I knew who was who based on Rick's steady adjusting of the knots.

Both slid hands down my back and over my ass, Max's pausing for a second to squeeze gently, then give me a sharp smack before moving lower to grip my thigh right above my knee.

Together they lifted my legs, bending them at the hips until I was in a seated position. Max touched my chin with his free hand and his mouth pressed against mine. I moaned around his probing tongue, my body already responding to the light touches he teased over my exposed skin. Rick's contact became only a background sensation compared to the sensual teasing of Max's fingers, very deliberate compared to the purely business-like sweep of Rick's ropes as he bound my thigh and tethered it to one of the steel rings above us.

Max toyed with my nipples one at a time, pinching and caressing over and over until I couldn't help but moan in response, then he moved lower, tracing the lines of the ropes down over my belly. He pulled my thigh wider and cupped my swollen pussy, sliding his palm down over my sensitive, throbbing flesh in a rough sweep, pausing with the heel of his palm at the top of my slit and rubbing in a slow circle.

My vision was clouded with pleasure, but he pulled away to allow Rick to step in and finish binding my other thigh. Then they were gone and I turned my head back and forth trying to track them, alarmed for a moment until I heard the sounds of movement behind me.

Rick came back around again. "Beautiful," he said, his tone hungry.

"Will I be able to see later?" I asked.

"No cameras up here. Tonight's about trust."

I tried to visualize how I must look anyway. Ropes were wrapped around and around my thighs, with tethers holding them up like a marionette's limbs. The angle of my shoulders caused my breasts to be thrust out. The hoops through my nipples were a constant presence with every breath. Rick flipped the lights off and even the dim light that came through the blind-fold disappeared.

"We're turning on colored lights," he said. We can

still see you, but you'll have a harder time tracing us visually through the blindfold."

A dark shape moved close. "You look beautiful," Max said, brushing his lips down the side of my jaw and sliding his hands over my skin. Something cool clinked against my nipple piercings. The sharp sting of a pair of clamps closing over my flesh made me wince at first, but soon enough the pain subsided into a steady throb.

Max's touch made me sway slightly on the ropes that I hung from and he took advantage of the movements to let me swing slowly into his touch and away again, each drift toward him pushing his fingertips further up my inner thighs. The rush of my utter helpless vulnerability made my pulse race, and the sensations that persisted on top of that had me aroused beyond imagining.

I turned my head about, trying desperately to track Max, already becoming discombobulated by the suspension and lack of sight. Only his steady touch kept me oriented, but my compass was royally screwed. My true North was Max and his touch. I couldn't help but sigh in ecstasy when his fingertips finally slid along my slick folds. This time he did more than tease, though. He sank his fingers deep into me, halting my swaying with a hooked motion inside me and pulling me toward him. The pressure of his fingers against that sweet, sensitive spot inside made me gasp, sure he must feel the way I heated and grew even slicker around him. I squirmed ineffectually against my bindings, but I didn't want to get away, I just wanted more.

"What next, baby?" he murmured in my ear. "Should I make you come now or do you want to draw this out? You can't move, so you have to tell me what you want. Remember, tonight's when you make the rules, but the next time we do this, you'll be gagged so you'd better make sure you tell us everything now."

His thumb flicked lightly over my clit and I nearly gave into his suggestion, but I knew I wanted more than just an orgasm. I wanted to feel everything. I shook my head. "Don't make me come yet. Make it last," I said. *Make it last forever, please.*

He nodded and pulled away from me, leaving me swinging and helpless.

For too long, I was left hanging, my arousal fully exposed with the ropes spreading me open and my legs tied wide. I could see nothing and could feel nothing but the flow of air across my naked skin.

I could hear them murmuring softly nearby, however. I just couldn't make out what they were saying. I listened as hard as I could, but the best I could hear was the word "want". The conversation stopped and a second later a gentle brush of a hand swept down my back from behind and something slick and warm pressed in the center of my exposed, spread ass cheeks.

"I made a promise to you yesterday," Rick said,

leaning close and whispering in my ear. His fingertips teased around and around tracing slick circles just at the edge of my sensitive, puckered opening. "Do you remember?"

"Yes," I said, still distracted wondering about their conversation, but quickly losing interest in it.

Max's hands returned to my waist from the front, making me jerk my head back around.

"Daddy?" I gasped.

"None other, baby," he said. "You doing all right?"

I sighed and leaned toward him in my darkness as much as I could. "I trust you," I said. "But this is a little scary."

"You can let go," he said. "Let yourself be a little scared. If you get a lot scared, you say so."

My breathing grew rapid at the bombardment of sensations. They began to slowly push me back and forth between them, not far enough for me to truly be swinging. I never completely left their contact. Rick kept a hand solidly against one of my hips and Max's fingers sank deep inside me again, stroking my tight channel with each surge toward him.

They spun me so it must be Rick facing me. He tugged at the chain that linked my breasts, making me hiss with the sting. A second later a pair of hot lips wrapped around one nipple and sucked, his tongue prodding the sensitive tip and flooding me with a combination of pleasure and pain. Then his fingers replaced Max's sliding between my slick folds.

"Christ, you're soaking wet. Do you think you're ready to get fucked yet, Casey?"

"Oh, God yes!"

"What about your tight little asshole? I think we need to break you in there, too."

He slid his slick fingers back farther, carrying the wet juices of my arousal to stroke again in tortuous circles around my asshole. When he moved his hand forward again, a whoosh of air hit my skin a split second before the stinging smack of something against my ass.

I cried out from the shock of it, my entire body writhing in my bindings in response.

It was the same sensation that had accompanied the leather flogger Max had used the day before. I'd loved it then, but this time it was harder, with the narrow bands of leather striking directly against my sensitive opening. I clenched, but strung up and spread out the way I was there was no escaping the whipping.

Max moved up close behind me and reached around, embracing me and murmuring into my ear, "I love looking at you like this, baby. Seeing how you react when I whip you makes me so fucking hard. Did that feel good when your pretty asshole stung?"

"Y-yes," I stuttered, so close to the point of mind-lessness I had trouble finding even the simplest words to speak.

He slid his hands down the front of my bound

torso, avoiding my pussy to grip my inner thighs and spread me a little wider.

"Time to let Rick have a little piece of you before it's my turn again," he said. His fingers tugged at the blindfold and pulled it off. When I opened my eyes I saw Rick striding toward me, his gaze intent on mine and his sweet lips parted to let his tongue sweep hungrily over his lower lip. It was the very same look he'd given me when we'd had our moment in the bedroom doorway earlier and my pussy clenched in need to have him inside me. His long cock was far from flaccid, jutting out in front of him like a battering ram.

"Are you ready for him, baby?" Max asked. "Or do I need to whip you until you are?"

"Oh, God," I moaned, my eyes fluttering closed at the idea. I tilted my head back against his cheek and whispered, "I want it all, please."

CHAPTER TWENTY-FIVE

"*Y*ou want it all, hmm? Rick said something about that. Maybe we should give it all to you now."

He left me swinging, walking around me to meet Rick, who paused barely within reach if I'd been able to use my arms at all. They gave each other the briefest look of understanding before Rick gripped Max by the back of his head, glanced at me with a triumphant smile, then slammed his lips against Max's mouth. Their hands clutched clumsily at each other, like they weren't quite sure what to do, but still wanted every bit of it. Max's fingers raked down Rick's torso until he cupped him between the legs. Rick jumped and pulled back from the kiss.

"We don't have to go there," he said, wide eyed.

I was just as wide-eyed watching, but didn't dare interrupt.

"Don't you want to?" Max asked. "It's always a nice shift when we want to satisfy a woman to the degree that we step out of our comfort zone."

"Jesus, yes. I'm just curious..." Rick paused and looked at me. "How much do you want, Case? We're at your mercy for the moment."

I suppressed the hysterical laughter that threatened to bubble up, covering it with irony instead. "I'm the one tied up and dangling from the ceiling and you're telling *me* you're at *my* mercy? I just want to know what you'd do if you weren't."

"Probably have a beer and go jerk off alone," Rick answered. Max responded with a laugh and a nod.

"The rules are different in this room," Max said. "They're what you make them."

"I want to see you touch each other. And then I want ... what I told Rick about."

Max nodded and tilted his head toward Rick again, their mouths locking together. Rick quivered with an odd tremor when Max's hand went between his legs again and gripped his cock, stroking it. My pussy throbbed even hotter when Rick followed his example, sliding his palm up Max's erection. He broke away from the kiss without removing his hand from Max's cock and looked at me.

"You've gotta say it out loud when you're ready, honey. We can't read your mind. Or are you just going to let us jerk each other off right in front of you?"

"N-no, I just want to see you pressed together.

Your dicks, I mean. And then I want you to fuck me like that."

They whispered a brief exchange before Max took over, holding both their hard flesh in his hands. He wrapped one hand around them both and squeezed. Rick let out a soft curse and looked at me, his gaze feverish. He reached toward me, sliding his hand up my bound thigh and pressing his fingers against my dripping cunt.

"You think your pussy's ready to take us both?"

My clit throbbed its own response under his teasing fingers. I was so ready I ached for it.

"Yes," I said. The quick breaths I took made the ropes dig tighter with ever inhalation and the chain stretched between my nipples made the clamps pinch. The sharp sensations were very apparent, but only aroused me more.

The pair of them parted after one more deep kiss and Max moved around to grip my hips from the back.

"You surprised me, Casey," Max said into my ear from behind. "Until Rick told me you wanted this, I thought I knew what to expect from you."

"Is this bad?" I asked breathlessly, my attention more focused on Rick's grip of my thighs from the front and his hot shaft aimed at the exposed, wet flesh between my thighs.

"It's never bad to push your boundaries. Sometimes you find out you love something you never thought you would. Now let's stretch that pretty little pussy of yours wide open."

Warm hands gripped the backs of my knees and I watched from beneath lowered lids as Rick slid between my spread legs. He reached one hand down and stroked me once, pressed his thick tip at my entrance and paused.

From behind, Max's tip pressed between my folds, too, and the pair of them pushed slowly in tandem.

"Ah!" I couldn't keep from crying out at the steady push and stretch. Alarming at first, but I was so wet and hot, my pussy easily let them in, accommodating their doubled girth in spite of how much my muscles protested at first. I felt dizzy from the effort to focus on the sensations and it was almost too much when Max grunted in my ear and the pair of them started moving.

"Christ, you're so tight," Rick said, his breath hot against my throat. "I want to feel you come like this, honey. You think you will?"

I thought I might never stop if I started, but there was nothing I wanted more. I could only stutter out an "uh-huh" when they pulled out and shoved deep again, their cocks stretching me further with each thrust. Every single nerve inside me lit up with the sheer, filling pressure of them, and to add insult, Rick slipped his hand between us and rubbed at my clit.

"Then let go, baby," Max said behind me. His hard stomach was pressed against my bound hands and I had just enough movement to dig my nails in. He reached around me and tugged the clips off my nipples. The abused buds screamed with tingling pain as the blood rushed back into them and I yelled out. My body betrayed me entirely, muscles clenching and bucking ineffectually as the combination of sensations became too much. They both fucked me harder and faster, holding me tight between them while I lost it, my only method of expression to cry louder as the orgasm shook me.

CHAPTER TWENTY-SIX

They exchanged a couple quick words I wasn't quite conscious of enough to comprehend and abruptly pulled out of me. I cried out in protest, but Rick squeezed my arm to still me.

"We're not done yet, honey, don't worry. Just need a short break. We need to last long enough to make sure you're good and satisfied."

He stepped away and I watched through a haze as he picked up a bottle of water from a cabinet against he far wall and took a long swallow. He brought it back to me and held the opening to my lips.

"Drink," he said. I complied and gulped greedily, unaware of how thirsty I'd become. The mouth of the bottle slipped and cold water dribbled down between my breasts. I let out a soft gasp when the trickle made it all the way down and ran between my thighs. "Your pussy need a little cool-off, too?" he asked and before I could answer he tipped the bottle and poured a measure over my pelvis. The cool water only partly soothed my still hot, throbbing flesh. It really only made me want more.

"Feels good," I said. "Fuck me again, please."

Rick tossed the empty bottle to the side and came forward. This time he didn't hesitate. He shoved his still hard cock deep into me, his mouth coming down onto mine at the same time.

"Still feel good?" he asked. He took advantage of the sway of the ropes to control my movements, pushing me back off his length with deliberate care before yanking me back toward him, impaling me on his stiff cock.

On one backward swing my ass was suddenly met with the stinging sweep of the flogger again—a swift crack followed by a lingering tickle as Max left it against my skin for a second before pulling back to deliver another blow. He only gave me a few strikes before his fingers hooked the ropes at my back and tugged me away from Rick, his cock slipping out of me and smacking against his belly before Max spun me around again.

Rick's hands at my hips caught me and held me still, his slick cock pressed against my sore asshole.

Max was between my thighs now, his hands cupping my face and his lips pressing against mine. I whimpered into his mouth, my body shaking from the combined sensations bombarding me in the aftermath of my mind blowing orgasm. Rick's cock pressed harder against my tight asshole, his voice harsh in my ear, begging me to relax.

"Let him in, baby," Max said. "Then you can have me." He aimed the tip of his cock between my swollen nether lips and teased it against my clit, our piercings clicking as they bumped each other.

I could only nod in response, my eyes fluttering closed with the combined pleasure and painful stretch of my asshole. Rick's cock pressed harder, breaching my slick opening and filling me inch by inch with his hard length. The harsh friction continued, transforming from pain to pleasure with each second, until his hips pressed against my ass and his steady panting gusted warm against my neck.

"Now," I cried. "Please fuck me now."

Max let out a low groan and swiftly shoved his cock deep into my pussy. Somehow I managed to stay conscious through the most intense pleasure of my life. Even the orgasm I'd just had couldn't compare. I could only close my eyes and succumb to their thick flesh pounding into me from both sides. One pair of hands gripped my hips—Max's I thought—while another hand toyed with my breasts and another slid between my thighs in front and rubbed my clit.

My pleasure felt suspended like my body, floating in mid-air, with no barriers between us.

"Let me feel you come again, baby. Tell me when you're close."

Some part of me didn't want to, though. The hot vibration of it was right there, pulsing in my core again like a tiny nuclear explosion frozen a split second before it went off. I wanted to remain suspended that way, floating in these amazing sensations, forever filled by them both, enslaved by pleasure. But Max wanted it and so I let myself give in.

"I am …" I said, followed by a series of breathy moans punctuated by their cocks thrusting and pushing my breath from my lungs.

"Me too," Rick murmured, his mouth against my neck. "Together, honey, I'm ready for you." His teeth sank into my shoulder, sending the spike of pain I needed to push me over the edge.

The bomb detonated, flooding my entire body with tingling, pulsing heat more intense than anything I'd experienced. I thought I cried out, but my voice was lost against the hungry pull of Max's lips and his tongue plunging between.

My hips twitched, muscles clenching as my reflexes struggled to buck into Max's thrusting pelvis, or back against Rick, chasing the pleasure, but Max's fingers dug hard into me, forcing me to remain still while the pair of them spent themselves inside me. Their cocks pulsed when they came, the throbbing sensation sweetly enhancing my own waning climax. My muscles clenched tightly around them both and I moaned again as both my invaded openings gripped them, wanting to draw out the pleasure just a little longer.

Even as my climax faded, they held me close, seeming as reluctant to let me go as I was for them to leave. Inevitably, they went, but only one at a time.

Max kissed me and slid out, stepping away only long enough to find a cloth to clean me up. I'd grown to love how attentive he was with me afterward, and sighed appreciatively at the delicate swipes over my tender flesh. Rick pulled out very slowly and began to untie me.

My head sagged and I let out a deep, satisfied sigh. The next few moments I spent in a daze, responding in monosyllables to the murmured questions from the two of them as Rick undid my bindings. Max carried me to the bed and laid me down and they both took turns massaging my limbs to make sure my blood was circulating. Everything tingled a little bit but nothing hurt aside from a tiny bit of soreness on my ass and the dull pain from where Rick had bitten me. I smiled at the thought that he'd owed me anyway.

When I saw them stand again and start to dress I raised up on my elbows and called out. "Wait, don't I get a choice about that?"

"About what, baby?" Max asked, confused.

"About you two putting on clothes so soon," I said, my mouth quirking up at the corner. "I kind of thought it was customary to snuggle after giving a girl a couple mind blowing orgasms, or am I wrong about that?"

Rick laughed and dropped his jeans to the floor. "She kind of has a point, man. What the hell were we thinking?" He walked back over to the bed and slid beneath the covers, wrapping me in his arms. Max followed, joining me on the other side.

He let his hand rest at my waist and kissed me on the forehead. "Like this?" he asked.

I bit my lip and shook my head. "No, turn over. Rick's got me, so let me get you."

He gave me a dubious look but did as I asked. With his back to me I shifted, pressed my bare breasts against his back and slung my leg over his hips from behind, then wrapped an arm around his chest. With my lips pressed against his ear I asked, "How's this?"

He clutched my hand in his larger one and held it to my chest. "Most comfortable I've been in my entire life."

I settled in with a sigh, enjoying the comforting skin-on-skin contact of both of them. Lethargy threatened to carry me to sleep, but I wasn't ready to just yet. My mind spun with all the questions I still had that I just didn't have the energy to ask just now. I did have the energy for one question.

"What happens next?" I asked.

I heard a low rumble and Rick's warm body pressed against me from behind. "Whatever we're in the mood for tomorrow."

Max tensed under my touch. "Tomorrow we have to go talk to your mother. After that … I hope you'll stay."

The mention of Mom made me clutch him tighter and his fingers clung to me as tightly as mine did to him. I could feel his heartbeat pounding hard in his chest.

"If you'll let me stay, I will. But do you mean here?"

Rick's breath gusted against my shoulder. "Where else, honey? This bed's built for us."If you enjoy Ophelia Bell's Taboo stories, you might enjoy these naughty tales...

Thank you for reading "Casey's Secrets"! If you loved it, please visit the retailer and leave a review!

And don't forget, subscribing to Ophelia's Dragon Beasties mailing list gets you **two free sexy dragon shifter stories** not available for sale anywhere and gives you direct access to updates on future stories by Ophelia.

Blackmailing Benjamin

PAYBACK NEVER FELT SO GOOD.

Kat's stepbrother, Ben, is one of the biggest jerks she's ever known. She's had to endure his ridicule for a decade, and to top it off, their parents seem to love him more. So when she catches him in a compromising position during a college frat party, she takes advantage of it, threatening to tell their parents his dirty little secrets in exchange for one tiny favor.

Ben gives in to Kat's blackmail, but in the process, Kat finds herself in a situation she never expected she'd be in. She definitely didn't expect to enjoy it so much. And she absolutely never expected to want more.

Buy Now.

Burying His Desires

Some things fit together better after they're broken.

A 3AM call is never good news, and for eighteen-year-old Britannia Vale, it's the worst. The man who raised her is on the other end, relaying a tragedy that will tear her entire world apart.

In the midst of grief, Britannia and Michael struggle to pick up the pieces, but the old pieces don't quite fit together they way they used to. She's no longer the little girl Michael helped her mother raise. Michael is still her hero, but looks at her in a way that incites overwhelming desires for the only man who can keep her whole in the aftermath of her mother's death. What's worse is that she might be the only person who can keep him whole, too.

How far will Britannia and Michael go to put the pieces back together?

Buy Now.

ABOUT OPHELIA BELL

Ophelia Bell loves a good bad-boy and especially strong women in her stories. Women who aren't apologetic about enjoying sex and bad boys who don't mind being with a woman who's in charge, at least on the surface, because pretty much anything goes in the bedroom.

Ophelia grew up on a rural farm in North Carolina and now lives in Los Angeles with her own tattooed bad-boy husband and six attention-whoring cats.

Subscribe to Ophelia's newsletter to get updates directly in your inbox. If newsletters aren't your thing, you can find her on social media.

http://opheliabell.com/subscribe

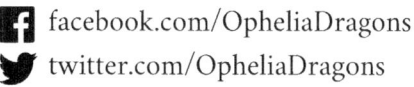

facebook.com/OpheliaDragons
twitter.com/OpheliaDragons

Dragon's Melody (a standalone dragon novel)

Immortal Dragons Series

Dragon Betrayed

Dragon Blues

Dragon Void

Dragon Splendor

Dragon Rebel

Dragon Guardian

Dragon Blessed

Dragon Equinox

Dragon Avenged

Immortal Dragons Box Sets:

Immortal Dragons: Books 1, 2, & 3 + Prequel

Immortal Dragons: Books 4-6 + Epilogue

Black Mountain Bears

Clawed

Bitten

Nailed

Stonetree Trilogy

Fate's Fools Series

Deva's Song (Fate's Fools Prequel)

Fate's Fools

Fool's Folly

Fool's Paradise

Fool's Errand

Nobody's Fool

Eye of the Hurricane

Fool's Bargain

April's Fools

Thieves of Fate

Aurora Champions Series

(Set in Milly Taiden's "Paranormal Dating Agency" world)

The Way to a Bear's Heart

Hot Wings

Triple Talons

Midnight Star

Once in a Dragon Moon

Rebel Lust Erotica

Casey's Secrets

Blackmailing Benjamin

Burying His Desires

Standalone Erotic Tales

After You

Out of the Cold

Printed in Great Britain
by Amazon

30894624R00111